The
Metamorphosis
&
Other Stories

Publications from
The Scheherazade Foundation

The Secrets of Scheherazade
An Ordered Experience
Tale of a Lantern & Other Stories
The Elephant & The Tortoise & Other Stories
The Monkey's Fiddle & Other Stories
Ghost of the Violet Well & Other Stories
Many Wise Fools & Other Stories
The Frog Prince & Other Stories
The Three Lemons & Other Stories
The Twelve-Headed Griffin & Other Stories
The Antelope Boy & Other Stories
Why the Fish Laughed & Other Stories
Two Cats & Other Stories
Three Stories
The Twilight of the Gods & Other Stories
The Son of Seven Queens & Other Stories
The Moon Maiden & Other Stories
The Metamorphosis & Other Stories
The Celestial Sisters & Other Stories
Tales from The Arabian Nights I
East of the Sun, West of the Moon & Other Stories
The Well at the End of the World & Other Stories

THE
METAMORPHOSIS
&
OTHER STORIES

Edited & Introduced by

TAHIR SHAH

The Scheherazade Foundation

The Scheherazade Foundation CIC
85 Great Portland Street
London
W1W 7LT
United Kingdom
www.SF.Charity
info@SF.Charity

First published by The Scheherazade Foundation CIC, 2023

THE METAMORPHOSIS
&
OTHER STORIES

Metamorphosis
Told in the Coffee House
Cyrus Adler & Allan Ramsay
Macmillan & Co.
1898

The Eta Maiden & the Hatamoto
Tales of Old Japan
Algernon Bertram Freeman-Mitford
Macmillan & Co.
1871

The Little Hunchback
The Arabian Nights Entertainments
Andrew Lang
Longmans, Green & Co.
1902

The Bride of the Evil One
English Folk-Tales in America
Elizabeth Johnston Cooke
1899

The Clever Thief
Tibetan Tales
F. Anton von Schiefner
Ballantine, Hanson & Co.
1882

The Swallow King's Rewards
Korean Tales
Horace Newton Allen
G. P. Putnam's Sons
1889

The Myddvai Legend
Welsh Folk-Lore
Elias Owen
Privately published
1887

The Happy Prince
The Happy Prince & Other Tales
Oscar Wilde
David Nutt Ltd.
1888

The Magic Turban
Tales of Folk & Fairies
Katharine Pyle
Little, Brown & Co.
1929

The various authors listed below assert the right to be identified as the Authors of the Work in accordance with the Copyright, Designs and Patents Act 1988. A CIP catalogue record for this title is available from the British Library.

ISBN 978-1-915311-29-0

Contents

Series Introduction

FROM EARLIEST CHILDHOOD, I was told stories.

Of course I was – most children are told stories.

After all, telling children stories is one of the foundations that makes their early experiences a childhood.

But as I think back to the first years of my own life, I find myself reeling from the sheer quantity of stories my infant ears took in.

Whereas other children my age were told stories for amusement, my parents (and the people they associated with) recounted the endless streams of tales for a different reason.

In their opinion, stories – and the ability to tell them – were part of an ancient alchemy... a way of processing complex ideas, of solving problems, and of developing the human mind.

My father, the writer and thinker Idries Shah, believed that folklore was the single most important breakthrough ever developed by the human species. The way he saw it, the rise of stories was as consequential as the development of the languages in which they were told.

He would say that, without stories and storytelling, humanity would never have evolved in the way that it has – and that the folktales, which form a bedrock of ancient societies, are more precious than any physical artefact unearthed on an archaeological dig.

As the years of my own childhood slipped by, I found myself unbothered to work out the hidden layers within treasuries of stories – what my father called 'instruction manuals to the world'. Like everyone else, I simply absorbed the individual tales, delighting in them.

And that's it – the key point, the genius of stories and storytelling.

It's a thing I only grasped in adulthood... something that fascinates me deeply.

In the same way you can jump into a car and drive across the country without giving a second thought to the engine or how it works, you can appreciate stories without understanding the hidden layers and devices that make them what they are.

Stories are all around us.

They're in the TV and movies we so adore, in the video games we play, and of course in the books we read. They're in newspapers and magazines, too; in the conversations we share with old friends, and with new ones. They're on our mobile phones, in aeroplanes, in submarines, and even in our dreams.

Our obsession with, and craving for, stories rests squarely with the way we are so absorbed by them, just as it does with the way we don't need to continually consider how and why they work.

Throughout my life, I've devoted an increasing amount of time to gathering stories from all corners of the world.

It began in my late teens, when I began to criss-cross the continents in a crazed preoccupation with folklore. I developed a first-hand love affair with societies that, over millennia, gave birth to their own astonishing traditions of stories and storytelling.

Most of the time, when reading or listening to stories, we forget that these tales have been shaped through the passage of time. Like pebbles in a river smoothed by rushing waters, they were honed through centuries of telling and retelling.

When I was twelve years old, my father published a masterwork, *World Tales*. The first edition was very large and featured hundreds of original illustrations. The book was unlike any that had come before, for it detailed the provenance and history of each story told.

At bedtime one night, he presented me with an advanced copy. For as long as I could remember, my father had been talking about the project.

Having an actual copy in my hands at last was thrilling beyond words.

Peering down at me sternly, my father said:

'This is far more than a book, Tahir Jan. It's the foundation stone of a great building... a building that *is* human culture. As you grow older, and as you go out into the world, you will understand that the folklores contained between the covers of *World Tales* have brought amusement and educated, and have solved problems when they were needed most of all.'

My father was right.

When I eventually headed out into the wilds of the world for the first time, I discovered the stories contained in *World Tales* for myself, along with a great many more. Just as he said, the stories published in his treasury were the warp and weft threads of society. Stories are the matrix on which culture itself is based – a framework that enables daily life to continue as smoothly as it does.

In this series of books, we have drawn together stories from all over the world. It's a mission begun decades ago by *World Tales*.

Some of the pieces will be known to you, and others will not.

Some will be easy to comprehend, while others will be challenging, or even nonsensical.

I'd now like to note something else…

The Occidental world seems to assume stories must appear in certain regimented ways – presented with a well-defined beginning, a middle, and an end. You know what I mean: the protagonist winning against all odds, and the happy ending to it all.

In the ancient tradition of teaching stories, the kind recounted for an eternity around campfires in the desert and in longhouses deep in the jungle, there's no such standardisation.

Rather, there's usually a hotchpotch of conflicting threads: stories without a straight linear narrative but with an underlying turbulence that gets the reader, or the listener, to sit up and think.

at The Scheherazade Foundation, we are preoccupied with the way we can extract knowledge from stories – either deliberately, or in a less structured way.

We hold the firm opinion that, in order to remove the marrow from the bone stories are best served up in the way as they were passed from one generation to the next throughout human history.

In this series, we have drawn together tales that were gathered in particular during the nineteenth and early twentieth centuries. Spanning a vast range of cultures, they offer an extraordinary glimpse into the societies from which they are drawn – societies that were often changed shortly afterwards by social upheaval, technologies, and war.

Indeed, the fact any of them were recorded at all is a thing of wonder.

Intriguingly, some of the tales will now appear dated because vocabulary and writing styles have altered. But the fact that they seem old-fashioned is of great interest – proof of the way stories are constantly changing and evolving from one era to the next.

Over the last thirty years, I've gathered hundreds of tales on my own journeys, most of them spoken directly into my ears by storytellers and fellow travellers, by wizened old men in the middle of nowhere, and by anyone else good enough to indulge my pleas.

On all those zigzagging adventures, one story sticks out, tantalising me whenever I turn it around my head.

It was called 'The Man Who Turned into a Cat'.

The reason I mention it here is not because it was an especially fine tale, but rather because, from that moment, it affected the way I perceive the world.

It was as though I were a lock and that, by hearing the tale, a key had been slipped into me and turned.

Since first receiving it, I've never been quite the same, my state of consciousness having been flipped inside out.

The fellow traveller who recounted 'The Man Who Turned into a Cat' was lost in shadow, no more than a fragment of his left cheek protruding shyly into the light.

We were sitting on low divans in a teahouse in the ancient Afghan city of Herat.

When the tale had been whispered, I sat there in silence for a long while.

'What have you done to me?' I asked after a long pause.

The fellow traveller offered half a smile.

'*I* didn't do anything,' he replied. 'It's the story that's affected you – a story that I myself first heard when I was a child playing in the orchards of Balkh.'

Peering into the shadow, my eyes widened.

'I don't understand,' I said feebly. 'After all, it's not an especially grand story. There wasn't even a jinn.'

The traveller's mouth eased out from the shadows.

Very slowly, it grinned.

'Tales containing the greatest sustenance for a soul speak in the softest voice,' he said.

Tahir Shah

The Metamorphosis

HUSSEIN AGHA WAS much troubled in spirit and mind. He had saved a large sum of money in order that he might make the pilgrimage to Mecca.

What troubled him was, that after having carefully provided for all the expenses of this long journey there still remained a few hundred piastres over and above. What was he to do with these? True, they could be distributed amongst the poor, but then, might not he, on his return, require the money for even a more meritorious purpose?

After much consideration, he decided that it was not Allah's wish that he should at once give this money in charity. On the other hand, he felt convinced that he should not give it to a brother for safekeeping, as he might be inspired, during Hussein's pilgrimage, to spend it on some charitable purpose.

After a time he thought of a kindly neighbour, and decided to leave his savings in the hands of this man, to whom Allah had been good, seeing that his possessions were great. After mature thought, he decided not to put temptation in the way of his neighbour. He therefore secured a jar, at the bottom of which he placed a small bag containing his surplus of wealth, and filled it with olives. This he carried to his neighbour, and begged him to take care of it for him. Ben Moïse of course consented, and Hussein Agha departed on his pilgrimage, contented.

On his return from the Holy Land, Hussein, now a Hadji, repaired to Ben Moïse and asked for his jar of olives, and at the same time presented Ben Moïse with a rosary of Yemen stones, in recognition of the service rendered him in the safe keeping of the olives, which, he said, were exceptionally palatable. Ben Moïse thanked him, and Hadji Hussein departed with his jar, well satisfied.

During the absence of Hussein Agha, it happened that Ben Moïse had some distinguished visitors, to whom, as is the Eastern custom, he served raki. Unfortunately, however, he had meze to offer, as is also the custom in the East. Ben Moïse bethought him of the olives and immediately went to the cellar, opened the jar, and extracted some of them, saying: 'Olives are not rare; Hussein will never know the difference if I replace them.'

The olives were found excellent, and Ben Moïse again and again helped his friends to them. Great was his surprise when he found that instead of olives, he brought forth a bag containing a quantity of gold. Ben Moïse could not understand this phenomenon, but appropriated the gold and held his peace.

Arriving home, poor Hussein Agha was distracted to find that his jar contained nothing but olives. Vainly did he protest to Ben Moïse.

'My friend,' he would reply, 'you gave me the jar, saying it contained olives. I believed you and kept the jar safe for you. Now you say that in the jar you had put some money together with the olives; perhaps you did, but is not that the jar you gave me? If, as you say, there was gold in the jar and it is now gone, all I can say is, the stronger has overcome the weaker, and that in this case the gold has either been converted into olives or into oil. What can I do? The jar you gave me I returned to you.'

Hadji Hussein admitted this, and fully appreciated that he had no case against the neighbour, so saying: 'Chok shai!' he returned to his home.

That night Hussein mingled in his prayers a vow to recover his gold at no matter what cost or trouble.

In his younger days, Hadji Hussein had been a pipe-maker, and many were the chi books of exceptional beauty that he had made. Go but to the potters' lane at Tophane, and the works of art displayed by the majority of them have been fashioned by the hands of Hussein. The art that had fed him for years was now to be the means of recovering his money.

Hadji Hussein daily met Ben Moïse but he never again referred to the money, and further, Hussein's sons were always in company with Ben Moïse's only son, a lad of ten.

Time passed, and Ben Moïse entirely forgot about the jar, olives, and gold; not so Hadji Hussein.

He had been working.

First, he had made an effigy of Ben Moïse. When he had completed this image to his satisfaction, he dressed it in the identical manner and costume the neighbour habitually wore. He then purchased a monkey. This monkey was kept in a cage opposite the effigy of Ben Moïse. Twice a day regularly the monkey's food was placed on the shoulders of the neighbour, and Hussein would open the cage, saying: 'Go to your father.'

At a bound, the monkey would plant himself on the shoulders of the neighbour, and would not be dislodged until its hunger had been satisfied.

In the meantime, Hadji Hussein and Ben Moïse were greater friends than ever, and their children were likewise playmates.

One day Hussein took Ben Moïse's son to his Harem and told him, much to the lad's joy, that he was to be their guest for a week. Later on, Ben Moïse called on Hadji Hussein to know the reason of his son's not returning as usual at sundown.

'Ah, my friend,' said Hussein, 'a great calamity has befallen you! Your son, alas! has been converted into a monkey, a furious monkey! So furious that I was compelled to put him into a cage. Come and see for yourself.'

No sooner did Ben Moïse enter the room in which the caged monkey was, than it set up a howl, not having had any food that day. Poor Ben Moïse was thunderstruck, and Hadji Hussein begged him to take the monkey away.

Next day Hussein was summoned to the court, the case of Ben Moïse was heard, and the Hadji was ordered to return the child at once. This he vowed he could not do, and to convince the judges he offered to bring the monkey caged as it was to the court, and, Inshallah, they would see for themselves that the child of the neighbour had been converted into a monkey.

This was ultimately agreed to, and the monkey was brought.

Hadji Hussein took special care to place the cage opposite Ben Moïse, and no sooner did the monkey catch sight of him than it set up a scream, and the judges said: 'Chok shai!'

Hussein Agha then opened the cage door, saying: 'Go to your father,' and the monkey with a bound and a yell embraced Ben Moïse, putting his head, in search of food, first on one shoulder of the neighbour and then on the other.

The judges were thunderstruck, and declared their incompetency to give judgment in such a case. Ben Moïse protested, saying that it was against the laws of nature for such a metamorphosis to take place, whereupon Hadji Hussein told the judges of an analogous instance of some gold pieces turning into olives, and called upon Ben Moïse to witness the veracity of his statement. The judges, much perplexed, dismissed the case, declaring that provision had not been made in the law for it, and there being no precedent to their knowledge they were incompetent to give judgment.

Leaving the court, Hadji Hussein informed Ben Moïse that there would still be pleasure and happiness in this world for him, provided he could reconvert the olives into gold.

Needless to add that Ben Moïse handed the money to Hadji Hussein, and the heir of Ben Moïse returned to his home none the worse for his transformation.

From: Told in the Coffee House

The Eta Maiden & the Hatamoto

ONCE UPON A time, some two hundred years ago, there lived at a place called Honjô, in Yedo, a Hatamoto named Takoji Genzaburô; his age was about twenty-four or twenty-five, and he was of extraordinary personal beauty.

His official duties made it incumbent on him to go to the Castle by way of the Adzuma Bridge, and here it was that a strange adventure befell him.

There was a certain Eta, who used to earn his living by going out every day to the Adzuma Bridge, and mending the sandals of the passers-by.

Whenever Genzaburô crossed the bridge, the Eta used always to bow to him. This struck him as rather strange; but one day when Genzaburô was out alone, without any retainers following him, and was passing the Adzuma Bridge, the thong of his sandal suddenly broke: this annoyed him very much; however, he recollected the Eta cobbler who always used to bow to him so regularly, so he went to the place where he usually sat, and ordered him to mend his sandal, saying to him: 'Tell me why it is that every time that I pass by this bridge, you salute me so respectfully.'

When the Eta heard this, he was put out of countenance, and for a while he remained silent; but at last taking courage, he said to Genzaburô, 'Sir, having been honoured with your commands, I am quite put to shame. I was originally a gardener, and used to go to your honour's house and lend a hand in trimming up the garden. In those days your honour was very young, and I myself little better than a child; and so I used to play with your honour, and received many kindnesses at your hands. My name, sir, is Chokichi. Since those days I have fallen by degrees info dissolute habits, and little by little have sunk to be the vile thing that you now see me.'

When Genzaburô heard this he was very much surprised, and, recollecting his old friendship for his playmate, was filled with pity, and said, 'Surely, surely, you have fallen very low. Now all you have to do is to persevere and use your utmost endeavours to find a means of escape from the class into which you have fallen, and become a wardsman again. Take this sum: small as it is, let it be a foundation for more to you.'

And with these words he took ten riyos out of his pouch and handed them to Chokichi, who at first refused to accept the present, but, when it was pressed upon him, received it with thanks. Genzaburô was leaving him to go home, when two wandering singing-girls came up and spoke to Chokichi; so Genzaburô looked to see what the two women were like.

One was a woman of some twenty years of age, and the other was a peerlessly beautiful girl of sixteen; she was neither too fat nor too thin, neither too tall nor too short; her face was oval, like a melon-seed, and her complexion fair and white; her eyes were narrow and bright, her teeth small and even; her nose was aquiline, and her mouth delicately formed, with lovely red lips; her eyebrows were long and fine; she had a profusion of long black hair; she spoke modestly, with a soft sweet voice; and when she smiled, two lovely dimples appeared in her cheeks; in all her movements she was gentle and refined.

Genzaburô fell in love with her at first sight; and she, seeing what a handsome man he was, equally fell in love with him; so that the woman that was with her, perceiving that they were struck with one another, led her away as fast as possible.

Genzaburô remained as one stupefied, and, turning to Chokichi, said, 'Are you acquainted with those two women who came up just now?'

'Sir,' replied Chokichi, 'those are two women of our people. The elder woman is called O Kuma, and the girl, who is only sixteen years old, is named O Koyo. She is the daughter of one Kihachi, a chief of the Etas. She is a very gentle girl, besides being so exceedingly pretty; and all our people are loud in her praise.'

When he heard this, Genzaburô remained lost in thought for a while, and then said to Chokichi, 'I want you to do something for me. Are you prepared to serve me in whatever respect I may require you?'

Chokichi answered that he was prepared to do anything in his power to oblige his honour. Upon this Genzaburô smiled and said, 'Well, then, I am willing to employ you in a certain matter; but as there are a great number of passers-by here, I will go and wait for you in a tea house at Hanakawado;

and when you have finished your business here, you can join me, and I will speak to you.'

With these words Genzaburô left him, and went off to the tea house.

When Chokichi had finished his work, he changed his clothes, and, hurrying to the tea house, inquired for Genzaburô, who was waiting for him upstairs. Chokichi went up to him, and began to thank him for the money which he had bestowed upon him. Genzaburô smiled, and handed him a wine cup, inviting him to drink, and said: 'I will tell you the service upon which I wish to employ you. I have set my heart upon that girl O Koyo, whom I met today upon the Adzuma Bridge, and you must arrange a meeting between us.'

When Chokichi heard these words, he was amazed and frightened, and for a while he made no answer.

At last he said: 'Sir, there is nothing that I would not do for you after the favours that I have received from you. If this girl were the daughter of any ordinary man, I would move heaven and earth to comply with your wishes; but for your honour, a handsome and noble Hatamoto, to take for his concubine the daughter of an Eta is a great mistake. By giving a little money you can get the handsomest woman in the town. Pray, sir, abandon the idea.'

Upon this Genzaburô was offended, and said: 'This is no matter for you to give advice in. I have told you to get me the girl, and you must obey.'

Chokichi, seeing that all that he could say would be of no avail, thought over in his mind how to bring about a meeting between Genzaburô and O Koyo, and replied: 'Sir,

I am afraid when I think of the liberty that I have taken. I will go to Kihachi's house, and will use my best endeavours with him that I may bring the girl to you. But for today, it is getting late, and night is coming on; so I will go and speak to her father tomorrow.'

Genzaburô was delighted to find Chokichi willing to serve him.

'Well,' said he, 'the day after tomorrow I will await you at the tea house at Oji, and you can bring O Koyo there. Take this present, small as it is, and do your best for me.'

With this he pulled out three riyos from his pocket and handed them to Chokichi. who declined the money with thanks, saying that he had already received too much, and could accept no more; but Genzaburô pressed him, adding, that if the wish of his heart were accomplished he would do still more for him. So Chokichi, in great glee at the good luck which had befallen him, began to revolve all sorts of schemes in his mind; and the two parted.

But O Koyo, who had fallen in love at first sight with Genzaburô on the Adzuma Bridge, went home and could think of nothing but him. Sad and melancholy she sat, and her friend O Kuma tried to comfort her in various ways; but O Koyo yearned, with all her heart, for Genzaburô; and the more she thought over the matter, the better she perceived that she, as the daughter of an Eta, was no match for a noble Hatamoto. And yet, in spite of this, she pined for him, and bewailed her own vile condition.

Now it happened that her friend O Kuma was in love with Chokichi, and only cared for thinking and speaking of him; one day, when Chokichi went to pay a visit at the house of

Kihachi the Eta chief, O Kuma, seeing him come, was highly delighted, and received him very politely; and Chokichi, interrupting her, said: 'O Kuma, I want you to answer me a question: where has O Koyo gone to amuse herself today?'

'Oh, you know the gentleman who was talking with you the other day, at the Adzuma Bridge? Well, O Koyo has fallen desperately in love with him, and she says that she is too low-spirited and out of sorts to get up yet.'

Chokichi was greatly pleased to hear this, and said to O Kuma: 'How delightful! Why, O Koyo has fallen in love with the very gentleman who is burning with passion for her, and who has employed me to help him in the matter. However, as he is a noble Hatamoto, and his whole family would be ruined if the affair became known to the world, we must endeavour to keep it as secret as possible.'

'Dear me!' replied O Kuma; 'when O Koyo hears this, how happy she will be, to be sure! I must go and tell her at once.'

'Stop!' said Chokichi, detaining her; 'if her father, Master Kihachi, is willing, we will tell O Koyo directly. You had better wait here a little until I have consulted him,' and with this, he went into an inner chamber to see Kihachi and, after talking over the news of the day, told him how Genzaburô had fallen passionately in love with O Koyo, and had employed him as a go-between. Then he described how he had received kindness at the hands of Genzaburô when he was in better circumstances, dwelt on the wonderful personal beauty of his lordship, and upon the lucky chance by which he and O Koyo had come to meet each other.

When Kihachi heard this story, he was greatly flattered, and said: 'I am sure I am very much obliged to you. For one of our daughters, whom even the common people despise and shun as a pollution, to be chosen as the concubine of a noble Hatamoto – what could be a greater matter for congratulation!'

So he prepared a feast for Chokichi, and went off at once to tell O Koyo the news. As for the maiden, who had fallen over head and ears in love, there was no difficulty in obtaining her consent to all that was asked of her.

Accordingly Chokichi, having arranged to bring the lovers together on the following day at Oji, was preparing to go and report the glad tidings to Genzaburô; but O Koyo, who knew that her friend O Kuma was in love with Chokichi, and thought that if she could throw them into one another's arms, they, on their side, would tell no tales about herself and Genzaburô, worked to such good purpose that she gained her point. At last Chokichi, tearing himself from the embraces of O Kuma, returned to Genzaburô, and told him how he had laid his plans so as, without fail, to bring O Koyo to him, the following day, at Oji, and Genzaburô, beside himself with impatience, waited for the morrow.

The next day Genzaburô, having made his preparations, and taking Chokichi with him, went to the tea house at Oji, and sat drinking wine, waiting for his sweetheart to come.

As for O Koyo, who was half in ecstasies, and half shy at the idea of meeting on this day the man of her heart's desire, she put on her holiday clothes, and went with O Kuma to Oji; and as they went out together, her natural beauty being enhanced by her smart dress, all the people turned round to look at her, and praise her pretty face. And so after a while, they arrived at Oji, and went into the tea house that had been agreed upon; and Chokichi, going out to meet them, exclaimed: 'Dear me, Miss O Koyo, his lordship has been all impatience waiting for you: pray make haste and come in.'

But, in spite of what he said, O Koyo, on account of her virgin modesty, would not go in. O Kuma, however, who was not quite so particular, cried out: 'Why, what is the meaning of this? As you've come here, O Koyo, it's a little late for you to be making a fuss about being shy. Don't be a little fool, but come in with me at once.'

And with these words she caught fast hold of O Koyo's hand, and, pulling her by force into the room, made her sit down by Genzaburô.

When Genzaburô saw how modest she was, he reassured her, saying: 'Come, what is there to be so shy about? Come a little nearer to me, pray.'

'Thank you, sir. How could I, who am such a vile thing, pollute your nobility by sitting by your side?'

And, as she spoke, the blushes mantled over her face; and the more Genzaburô looked at her, the more beautiful she appeared in his eyes, and the more deeply he became enamoured of her charms. In the meanwhile he called for wine and fish, and all four together made a feast of it.

When Chokichi and O Kuma saw how the land lay, they retired discreetly into another chamber, and Genzaburô and O Koyo were left alone together, looking at one another.

'Come,' said Genzaburô, smiling, 'hadn't you better sit a little closer to me?'

'Thank you, sir; really I'm afraid.'

But Genzaburô, laughing at her for her idle fears, said: 'Don't behave as if you hated me.'

'Oh, dear! I'm sure I don't hate you, sir. That would be very rude; and, indeed, it's not the case. I loved you when I first saw you at the Adzuma Bridge, and longed for you with all my heart; but I knew what a despised race I belonged to, and that I was no fitting match for you, and so I tried to be resigned. But I am very young and inexperienced, and so I could not help thinking of you, and you alone; and then Chokichi came, and when I heard what you had said about me, I thought, in the joy of my heart, that it must be a dream of happiness.'

And as she spoke these words, blushing timidly, Genzaburô was dazzled with her beauty, and said:v'Well, you're a clever child. I'm sure, now, you must have some handsome young lover of your own, and that is why you don't care to come and drink wine and sit by me. Am I not right, eh?'

'Ah, sir, a nobleman like you is sure to have a beautiful wife at home; and then you are so handsome that, of course, all the pretty young ladies are in love with you.'

'Nonsense! Why, how clever you are at flattering and paying compliments! A pretty little creature like you was just made to turn all the men's heads – a little witch.'

'Ah! those are hard things to say of a poor girl! Who could think of falling in love with such a wretch as I am? Now, pray tell me all about your own sweetheart: I do so long to hear about her.'

'Silly child! I'm not the sort of man to put thoughts into the heads of fair ladies. However, it is quite true that there is someone whom I want to marry.'

At this O Koyo began to feel jealous.

'Ah!' said she, 'how happy that someone must be! Do, pray, tell me the whole story.'

And a feeling of jealous spite came over her, and made her quite unhappy. Genzaburô laughed as he answered: 'Well, that someone is yourself, and nobody else. There!' and as he spoke, he gently tapped the dimple on her cheek with his finger; and O Koyo's heart beat so, for very joy, that, for a little while, she remained speechless.

At last, she turned her face towards Genzaburô, and said: 'Alas! your lordship is only trifling with me, when you know that what you have just been pleased to propose is the darling wish of my heart. Would that I could only go into your house as a maid-servant, in any capacity, however mean, that I might daily feast my eyes on your handsome face!'

'Ah! I see that you think yourself very clever at hoaxing men, and so you must needs tease me a little;' and, as he spoke, he took her hand, and drew her close up to him, and she, blushing again, cried: 'Oh! pray wait a moment, while I shut the sliding doors.'

'Listen to me, O Koyo! I am not going to forget the promise which I made you just now; nor need you be afraid of my harming you; but take care that you do not deceive me.'

'Indeed, sir, the fear is rather that you should set your heart on others; but, although I am no fashionable lady, take pity on me, and love me well and long.'

'Of course! I shall never care for another woman but you.'

'Pray, pray, never forget those words that you have just spoken.'

'And now,' replied Genzaburô, 'the night is advancing, and, for today, we must part; but we will arrange matters, so as to meet again in this tea-house. But, as people would make remarks if we left the tea house together, I will go out first.'

And so, much against their will, they tore themselves from one another, Genzaburô returning to his house, and O Koyo going home, her heart filled with joy at having found the man for whom she had pined; and from that day forth they used constantly to meet in secret at the tea-house; and Genzaburô, in his infatuation, never thought that the matter must surely become notorious after a while, and that he himself would be banished, and his family ruined: he only took care for the pleasure of the moment.

Now Chokichi, who had brought about the meeting between Genzaburô and his love, used to go every day to the tea house at Oji, taking with him O Koyo; and Genzaburô neglected all his duties for the pleasure of these secret meetings. Chokichi saw this with great regret, and thought to himself that if Genzaburô gave himself up entirely to pleasure, and laid aside his duties, the secret would certainly be made public, and Genzaburô would bring ruin on himself and his family; so he began to devise some plan by which he might separate them, and plotted as eagerly to estrange them as he had formerly done to introduce them to one another.

At last he hit upon a device which satisfied him. Accordingly one day he went to O Koyo's house, and, meeting her father Kihachi, said to him: 'I've got a sad piece of news to tell you. The family of my lord Genzaburô have been complaining bitterly of his conduct in carrying on his relationship with your daughter, and of the ruin which exposure would bring upon the whole house; so they have been using their influence to persuade him to hear reason, and give up the connection.

'Now his lordship feels deeply for the damsel, and yet he cannot sacrifice his family for her sake. For the first time, he has become alive to the folly of which he has been guilty, and, full of remorse, he has commissioned me to devise some stratagem to break off the affair. Of course, this has taken me by surprise; but as there is no gainsaying the right of the case, I have had no option but to promise obedience: this promise I have come to redeem; and now, pray, advise your daughter to think no more of his lordship.'

When Kihachi heard this he was surprised and distressed, and told O Koyo immediately; and she, grieving over the sad news, took no thought either of eating or drinking, but remained gloomy and desolate.

In the meanwhile, Chokichi went off to Genzaburô's house, and told him that O Koyo had been taken suddenly ill, and could not go to meet him, and begged him to wait patiently until she should send to tell him of her recovery. Genzaburô, never suspecting the story to be false, waited for thirty days, and still Chokichi brought him no tidings of O Koyo. At last he met Chokichi, and besought him to arrange a meeting for him with O Koyo.

'Sir,' replied Chokichi, 'she is not yet recovered; so it would be difficult to bring her to see your honour. But I have been thinking much about this affair, sir. If it becomes public, your honour's family will be plunged in ruin. I pray you, sir, to forget all about O Koyo.'

'It's all very well for you to give me advice,' answered Genzaburô, surprised; 'but, having once bound myself to O Koyo, it would be a pitiful thing to desert her; I therefore implore you once more to arrange that I may meet her.'

However, he would not consent upon any account; so Genzaburô returned home, and, from that time forth, daily entreated Chokichi to bring O Koyo to him, and, receiving nothing but advice from him in return, was very sad and lonely.

One day Genzaburô, intent on ridding himself of the grief he felt at his separation from O Koyo, went to the Yoshiwara, and, going into a house of entertainment, ordered a feast to be prepared, but, in the midst of gaiety, his heart yearned all the while for his lost love, and his merriment was but mourning in disguise. At last the night wore on; and as he was retiring along the corridor, he saw a man of about forty years of age, with long hair, coming towards him, who, when he saw Genzaburô, cried out, 'Dear me! why this must be my young lord Genzaburô who has come out to enjoy himself.'

Genzaburô thought this rather strange; but, looking at the man attentively, recognized him as a retainer whom he had had in his employ the year before, and said: 'This is a curious meeting: pray, what have you been about since you left my service? At any rate, I may congratulate you on being well and strong. Where are you living now?'

'Well, sir, since I parted from you I have been earning a living as a fortune-teller at Kanda, and have changed my name to Kaji Sazen. I am living in a poor and humble house; but if your lordship, at your leisure, would honour me with a visit.'

'Well, it's a lucky chance that has brought us together, and I certainly will go and see you; besides, I want you to do something for me. Shall you be at home the day after tomorrow?'

'Certainly, sir, I shall make a point of being at home.'

'Very well, then, the day after tomorrow I will go to your house.'

'I shall be at your service, sir. And now, as it is getting late, I will take my leave for tonight.'

'Good night, then. We shall meet the day after tomorrow.'

And so the two parted, and went their separate ways to rest.

On the appointed day Genzaburô made his preparations, and went in disguise, without any retainers, to call upon Sazen, who met him at the porch of his house, and said, 'This is a great honour! My lord Genzaburô is indeed welcome. My house is very mean, but let me invite your lordship to come into an inner chamber.'

'Pray,' replied Genzaburô, 'don't make any ceremony for me. Don't put yourself to any trouble on my account.'

And so he passed in, and Sazen called to his wife to prepare wine and condiments; and they began to feast. At last Genzaburô, looking Sazen in the face, said, 'There is a service which I want you to render me – a very secret service; but as if you were to refuse me, I should be put to shame, before I tell you what that service is, I must know whether you are willing to assist me in anything that I may require of you.'

'Yes; if it is anything that is within my power, I am at your disposal.'

'Well, then,' said Genzaburô, greatly pleased, and drawing ten riyos from his bosom, 'this is but a small present to make to you on my first visit, but pray accept it.'

'No, indeed! I don't know what your lordship wishes of me; but, at any rate, I cannot receive this money. I really must beg your lordship to take it back again.'

But Genzaburô pressed it upon him by force, and at last he was obliged to accept the money. Then Genzaburô told him the whole story of his love with O Koyo – how he had first met her and fallen in love with her at the Adzuma Bridge; how Chokichi had introduced her to him at the tea-house at Oji, and then when she fell ill, and he wanted to see her again, instead of bringing her to him, had only given him good advice; and so Genzaburô drew a lamentable picture of his state of despair.

Sazen listened patiently to his story, and, after reflecting for a while, replied, 'Well, sir, it's not a difficult matter to set right: and yet it will require some little management. However, if your lordship will do me the honour of coming to see me again the day after tomorrow, I will cast about me in the meanwhile, and will let you know then the result of my deliberations.'

When Genzaburô heard this he felt greatly relieved, and, recommending Sazen to do his best in the matter, took his leave and returned home. That very night Sazen, after thinking over all that Genzaburô had told him, laid his plans accordingly, and went off to the house of Kihachi, the Eta chief, and told him the commission with which he had been entrusted.

Kihachi was of course greatly astonished, and said, 'Some time ago, sir, Chokichi came here and said that my lord Genzaburô, having been rebuked by his family for his profligate behaviour, had determined to break off his connection with my daughter. Of course I knew that the daughter of an Eta was no fitting match for a nobleman; so when Chokichi came and told me the errand upon which he had been sent, I had no alternative but to announce to my daughter that she must give up all thought of his lordship. Since that time she has been fretting and pining and starving for love. But when I tell her what you have just said, how glad and happy she will be! Let me go and talk to her at once.'

And with these words, he went to O Koyo's room; and when he looked upon her thin wasted face, and saw how sad she was, he felt more and more pity for her, and said, 'Well, O Koyo, are you in better spirits today? Would you like something to eat?'

'Thank you, I have no appetite.'

'Well, at any rate, I have some news for you that will make you happy. A messenger has come from my lord Genzaburô, for whom your heart yearns.'

At this O Koyo, who had been crouching down like a drooping flower, gave a great start, and cried out, 'Is that really true? Pray tell me all about it as quickly as possible.'

'The story which Chokichi came and told us, that his lordship wished to break off the connection, was all an invention. He has all along been wishing to meet you, and constantly urged Chokichi to bring you a message from him. It is Chokichi who has been throwing obstacles in the way. At last his lordship has secretly sent a man, called Kaji Sazen, a fortune-teller, to arrange an interview between you. So now, my child, you may cheer up, and go to meet your lover as soon as you please.'

When O Koyo heard this, she was so happy that she thought it must all be a dream, and doubted her own senses.

Kihachi in the meanwhile rejoined Sazen in the other room, and, after telling him of the joy with which his daughter had heard the news, put before him wine and other delicacies.

'I think,' said Sazen, 'that the best way would be for O Koyo to live secretly in my lord Genzaburô's house; but as it will never do for all the world to know of it, it must be managed very quietly; and further, when I get home, I must think out some plan to lull the suspicions of that fellow Chokichi, and let you know my idea by letter. Meanwhile O Koyo had better come home with me tonight: although she is so terribly out of spirits now, she shall meet Genzaburô the day after tomorrow.'

Kihachi reported this to O Koyo; and as her pining for Genzaburô was the only cause of her sickness, she recovered her spirits at once, and, saying that she would go with Sazen immediately, joyfully made her preparations.

Then Sazen, having once more warned Kihachi to keep the matter secret from Chokichi, and to act upon the letter which he should send him, returned home, taking with him O Koyo; and after O Koyo had bathed and dressed her hair, and painted herself and put on beautiful clothes, she came out looking so lovely that no princess in the land could vie with her; and Sazen, when he saw her, said to himself that it was no wonder that Genzaburô had fallen in love with her; then, as it was getting late, he advised her to go to rest, and, after showing her to her apartments, went to his own room and wrote his letter to Kihachi, containing the scheme which he had devised.

When Kihachi received his instructions, he was filled with admiration at Sazen's ingenuity, and, putting on an appearance of great alarm and agitation, went off immediately to call on Chokichi, and said to him: 'Oh, Master Chokichi, such a terrible thing has happened! Pray, let me tell you all about it.'

'Indeed! What can it be?'

'Oh! Sir,' answered Kihachi, pretending to wipe away his tears, 'my daughter O Koyo, mourning over her separation from my lord Genzaburô, at first refused all sustenance, and remained nursing her sorrows until, last night, her woman's heart failing to bear up against her great grief, she drowned herself in the river, leaving behind her a paper on which she had written her intention.'

When Chokichi heard this, he was thunderstruck, and exclaimed, 'Can this really be true! And when I think that it was I who first introduced her to my lord, I am ashamed to look you in the face.'

'Oh, say not so: misfortunes are the punishment due for our misdeeds in a former state of existence. I bear you no ill will. This money which I hold in my hand was my daughter's; and in her last instructions she wrote to beg that it might be given, after her death, to you, through whose intervention she became allied with a nobleman: so please

29

accept it as my daughter's legacy to you;' and as he spoke, he offered him three riyos.

'You amaze me!' replied the other. 'How could I, above all men, who have so much to reproach myself with in my conduct towards you, accept this money?'

'Nay; it was my dead daughter's wish. But since you reproach yourself in the matter when you think of her, I will beg you to put up a prayer and to cause masses to be said for her.'

At last, Chokichi, after much persuasion, and greatly to his own distress, was obliged to accept the money; and when Kihachi had carried out all Sazen's instructions, he returned home, laughing in his sleeve.

Chokichi was sorely grieved to hear of O Koyo's death, and remained thinking over the sad news; when all of a sudden looking about him, he saw something like a letter lying on the spot where Kihachi had been sitting, so he picked it up and read it; and, as luck would have it, it was the very letter which contained Sazen's instructions to Kihachi, and in which the whole story which had just affected him so much was made up.

When he perceived the trick that had been played upon him, he was very angry, and exclaimed, 'To think that I should have been so hoaxed by that hateful old dotard, and such a fellow as Sazen! And Genzaburô, too! – out of gratitude for the favours which I had received from him in old days, I faithfully gave him good advice, and all in vain. Well, they've gulled me once; but I'll be even with them yet, and hinder their game before it is played out!'

And so he worked himself up into a fury, and went off secretly to prowl about Sazen's house to watch for O Koyo, determined to pay off Genzaburô and Sazen for their conduct to him.

In the meanwhile Sazen, who did not for a moment suspect what had happened, when the day which had been fixed upon by him and Genzaburô arrived, made O Koyo put on her best clothes, smartened up his house, and got ready a feast against Genzaburô's arrival. The latter came punctually to his time, and, going in at once, said to the fortune-teller, 'Well, have you succeeded in the commission with which I entrusted you?'

At first Sazen pretended to be vexed at the question, and said, 'Well, sir, I've done my best; but it's not a matter which can be settled in a hurry. However, there's a young lady of high birth and wonderful beauty upstairs, who has come here secretly to have her fortune told; and if your lordship would like to come with me and see her, you can do so.'

But Genzaburô, when he heard that he was not to meet O Koyo, lost heart entirely, and made up his mind to go home again. Sazen, however, pressed him so eagerly, that at last he went upstairs to see this vaunted beauty; and Sazen, drawing aside a screen, showed him O Koyo, who was sitting there. Genzaburô gave a great start, and, turning to Sazen, said, 'Well, you certainly are a first-rate hand at keeping up a hoax. However, I cannot sufficiently praise the way in which you have carried out my instructions.'

'Pray, don't mention it, sir. But as it is a long time since you have met the young lady, you must have a great deal to say to one another; so I will go downstairs, and, if you want anything, pray call me.'

And so he went downstairs and left them.

Then Genzaburô, addressing O Koyo, said, 'Ah! it is indeed a long time since we met. How happy it makes me to see you again! Why, your face has grown quite thin. Poor thing! Have you been unhappy?'

And O Koyo, with the tears starting from her eyes for joy, hid her face; and her heart was so full that she could not speak. But Genzaburô, passing his hand gently over her head and back, and comforting her, said, 'Come, sweetheart, there is no need to sob so. Talk to me a little, and let me hear your voice.'

At last O Koyo raised her head and said, 'Ah! When I was separated from you by the tricks of Chokichi, and thought that I should never meet you again, how tenderly I thought of you! I thought I should have died, and waited for my hour to come, pining all the while for you. And when at last, as I lay between life and death, Sazen came with a message from you, I thought it was all a dream.'

And as she spoke, she bent her head and sobbed again; and in Genzaburô's eyes she seemed more beautiful than ever, with her pale, delicate face; and he loved her better than before. Then she said, 'If I were to tell you all I have suffered until today, I should never stop.'

'Yes,' replied Genzaburô, 'I too have suffered much;' and so they told one another their mutual griefs, and from that day forth they constantly met at Sazen's house.

One day, as they were feasting and enjoying themselves in an upper storey in Sazen's house, Chokichi came to the house and said, 'I beg pardon; but does one Master Sazen live here?'

'Certainly, sir: I am Sazen, at your service. Pray where are you from?'

'Well, sir, I have a little business to transact with you. May I make so bold as to go in?' And with these words, he entered the house.

'But who and what are you?' said Sazen.

'Sir, I am an Eta; and my name is Chokichi. I beg to bespeak your goodwill for myself: I hope we may be friends.'

Sazen was not a little taken aback at this; however, he put on an innocent face, as though he had never heard of Chokichi before, and said, 'I never heard of such a thing! Why, I thought you were some respectable person; and you have the impudence to tell me that your name is Chokichi, and that you're one of those accursed Etas. To think of such a shameless villain coming and asking to be friends with me, forsooth! Get you gone! The quicker, the better: your presence pollutes the house.'

Chokichi smiled contemptuously, as he answered, 'So you deem the presence of an Eta in your house a pollution – eh? Why, I thought you must be one of us.'

'Insolent knave! Begone as fast as possible.'

'Well, since you say that I defile your house, you had better get rid of O Koyo as well. I suppose she must equally be a pollution to it.'

This put Sazen rather in a dilemma; however, he made up his mind not to show any hesitation, and said, 'What are you talking about? There is no O Koyo here; and I never saw such a person in my life.'

Chokichi quietly drew out of the bosom of his dress the letter from Sazen to Kihachi, which he had picked up a few days before, and, showing it to Sazen, replied, 'If you wish to dispute the genuineness of this paper, I will report the whole matter to the Governor of Yedo; and Genzaburô's family will be ruined, and the rest of you who are parties in this affair will come in for your share of trouble. Just wait a little.'

And as he pretended to leave the house, Sazen, at his wits' end, cried out, 'Stop! stop! I want to speak to you. Pray, stop and listen quietly. It is quite true, as you said, that O Koyo is in my house; and really your indignation is perfectly just. Come! let us talk over matters a little. Now you yourself were originally a respectable man; and although you have fallen in life, there is no reason why your disgrace should last forever.

'All that you want in order to enable you to escape out of this fraternity of Etas is a little money. Why should you not get this from Genzaburô, who is very anxious to keep his intrigue with O Koyo secret?'

Chokichi laughed disdainfully. 'I am ready to talk with you; but I don't want any money. All I want is to report the affair to the authorities, in order that I may be revenged for the fraud that was put upon me.'

'Won't you accept twenty-five riyos?'

'Twenty-five riyos! No, indeed! I will not take a fraction less than a hundred; and if I cannot get them I will report the whole matter at once.'

Sazen, after a moment's consideration, hit upon a scheme, and answered, smiling, 'Well, Master Chokichi, you're a fine fellow, and I admire your spirit. You shall have the hundred riyos you ask for; but, as I have not so much money by me at present, I will go to Genzaburô's house and fetch it. It's getting dark now, but it's not very late; so I'll trouble you to come with me, and then I can give you the money tonight.'

Chokichi consenting to this, the pair left the house together.

Now Sazen, who as a Rônin wore a long dirk in his girdle, kept looking out for a moment when Chokichi should be off his guard, in order to kill him; but Chokichi kept his eyes open, and did not give Sazen a chance.

At last Chokichi, as ill-luck would have it, stumbled against a stone and fell; and Sazen, profiting by the chance, drew his dirk and stabbed him in the side; and as Chokichi, taken by surprise, tried to get up, he cut him severely over the head, until at last he fell dead. Sazen then looking around him, and seeing, to his great delight, that there was no one near, returned home.

The following day, Chokichi's body was found by the police; and when they examined it, they found nothing upon it save a paper, which they read, and which proved to be the very letter which Sazen had sent to Kihachi, and which Chokichi had picked up.

The matter was immediately reported to the governor, and, Sazen having been summoned, an investigation was held.

Sazen, cunning and bold murderer as he was, lost his self-possession when he saw what a fool he had been not to get back from Chokichi the letter which he had written, and, when he was put to a rigid examination under torture, confessed that he had hidden O Koyo at Genzaburô's instigation, and then killed Chokichi, who had found out the secret.

Upon this the governor, after consulting about Genzaburô's case, decided that, as he had disgraced his position as a Hatamoto by contracting an alliance with the daughter of an Eta, his property should be confiscated, his family blotted out, and himself banished.

As for Kihachi, the Eta chief, and his daughter O Koyo, they were handed over for punishment to the chief of the Etas, and by him they too were banished; while Sazen, against whom the murder of Chokichi had been fully proved, was executed according to law.

From: Tales of Old Japan

The Little Hunchback

IN THE KINGDOM of Kashgar, which is, as everybody knows, situated on the frontiers of Great Tartary, there lived long ago a tailor and his wife who loved each other very much.

One day, when the tailor was hard at work, a little hunchback came and sat at the entrance of the shop, and began to sing and play his tambourine.

The tailor was amused with the antics of the fellow and thought he would take him home to divert his wife. The hunchback having agreed to his proposal, the tailor closed his shop and they set off together.

When they reached the house they found the table ready laid for supper, and in a very few minutes all three were sitting before a beautiful fish which the tailor's wife had cooked with her own hands. But unluckily, the hunchback happened to swallow a large bone, and, in spite of all the tailor and his wife could do to help him, died of suffocation in an instant.

Besides being very sorry for the poor man, the tailor and his wife were very much frightened on their own account, for if the police came to hear of it the worthy couple ran the risk of being thrown into prison for wilful murder. In order to prevent this dreadful calamity they both set about inventing some plan which would throw suspicion on someone else, and at last they made up their minds that they could do no better than select a neighbourhood doctor as the author of the crime.

So the tailor picked up the hunchback by his head while his wife took his feet and carried him to the doctor's house. Then they knocked at the door, which opened straight on to a steep staircase. A servant soon appeared, feeling her way down the dark staircase and inquired what they wanted.

'Tell your master,' said the tailor, 'that we have brought a very sick man for him to cure; and,' he added, holding out some money, 'give him this in advance, so that he may not feel he is wasting his time.'

The servant remounted the stairs to give the message to the doctor, and the moment she was out of sight the tailor and his wife carried the body swiftly after her, propped it up at the top of the staircase, and ran home as fast as their legs could carry them.

Now the doctor was so delighted at the news of a patient (for he was young, and had not many of them), that he was transported with joy.

'Get a light,' he called to the servant, 'and follow me as fast as you can!' and rushing out of his room he ran towards the staircase. There he nearly fell over the body of the hunchback, and without knowing what it was gave it such a kick that it rolled right to the bottom, and very nearly dragged the doctor after it.

'A light! A light!' he cried again, and when it was brought and he saw what he had done he was almost beside himself with terror.

'Holy Moses!' he exclaimed, 'why did I not wait for the light? I have killed the sick man whom they brought me; and if the sacred Ass of Esdras does not come to my aid I am lost! It will not be long before I am led to jail as a murderer.'

Agitated though he was, and with reason, the doctor did not forget to shut the house door, lest some passersby might chance to see what had happened. He then took up the corpse and carried it into his wife's room, nearly driving her crazy with fright.

'It is all over with us!' she wailed, 'if we cannot find some means of getting the body out of the house. Once let the sun rise and we can hide it no longer! How were you driven to commit such a terrible crime?'

'Never mind that,' returned the doctor, the thing is to find a way out of it.'

For a long while the doctor and his wife continued to turn over in their minds a way of escape, but could not find any that seemed good enough. At last the doctor gave it up altogether and resigned himself to bear the penalty of his misfortune.

But his wife, who had twice his brains, suddenly exclaimed, 'I have thought of something! Let us carry the body on the roof of the house and lower it down the chimney of our neighbour the Mussulman.'

Now this Mussulman was employed by the sultan, and furnished his table with oil and butter. Part of his house was occupied by a great storeroom, where rats and mice held high revel.

The doctor jumped at his wife's plan, and they took up the hunchback, and passing cords under his armpits they let him down into the purveyor's bedroom so gently that he really seemed to be leaning against the wall. When they felt he was touching the ground they drew up the cords and left him.

Scarcely had they got back to their own house when the purveyor entered his room. He had spent the evening at a wedding feast, and had a lantern in his hand. In the dim light it cast he was astonished to see a man standing in his chimney, but being naturally courageous he seized a stick and made straight for the supposed thief.

'Ah!' he cried, 'so it is you, and not the rats and mice, who steal my butter. I'll take care that you don't want to come back!'

So saying he struck him several hard blows. The corpse fell on the floor, but the man only redoubled his blows, till at length it occurred to him it was odd that the thief should lie so still and make no resistance. Then, finding he was quite dead, a cold fear took possession of him.

'Wretch that I am,' said he, 'I have murdered a man. Ah, my revenge has gone too far. Without the help of Allah I am undone! Cursed be the goods which have led me to my ruin.'

And already he felt the rope round his neck.

But when he had got over the first shock he began to think of some way out of the difficulty, and seizing the hunchback in his arms he carried him out into the street, and leaning him against the wall of a shop he stole back to his own house, without once looking behind him.

A few minutes before the sun rose, a rich Christian merchant, who supplied the palace with all sorts of necessaries, left his house, after a night of feasting, to go to the bath. Though he was very drunk, he was yet sober enough to know that the dawn was at hand, and that all good Mussulmen would shortly be going to prayer.

So he hastened his steps lest he should meet someone on his way to the mosque, who, seeing his condition, would send him to prison as a drunkard. In his haste he jostled against the hunchback, who fell heavily upon him, and the merchant, thinking he was being attacked by a thief, knocked him down with one blow of his fist. He then called loudly for help, beating the fallen man all the while.

The chief policeman of the quarter came running up, and found a Christian ill-treating a Mussulman.

'What are you doing?' he asked indignantly.

'He tried to rob me,' replied the merchant, 'and very nearly choked me.'

'Well, you have had your revenge,' said the man, catching hold of his arm. 'Come, be off with you!'

As he spoke he held out his hand to the hunchback to help him up, but the hunchback never moved.

'Oho!' he went on, looking closer, 'so this is the way a Christian has the impudence to treat a Mussulman!' and seizing the merchant in a firm grasp he took him to the inspector of police, who threw him into prison till the judge should be out of bed and ready to attend to his case. All this brought the merchant to his senses, but the more he thought of it the less he could understand how the hunchback could have died merely from the blows he had received.

The merchant was still pondering on this subject when he was summoned before the chief of police and questioned about his crime, which he could not deny. As the hunchback

41

was one of the sultan's private jesters, the chief of police resolved to defer sentence of death until he had consulted his master. He went to the palace to demand an audience, and told his story to the sultan, who only answered, 'There is no pardon for a Christian who kills a Mussulman. Do your duty.'

So the chief of police ordered a gallows to be erected, and sent criers to proclaim in every street in the city that a Christian was to be hanged that day for having killed a Mussulman.

When all was ready the merchant was brought from prison and led to the foot of the gallows. The executioner knotted the cord firmly around the unfortunate man's neck and was just about to swing him into the air, when the sultan's purveyor dashed through the crowd, and cried, panting, to the hangman, 'Stop, stop, don't be in such a hurry. It was not he who did the murder, it was I.'

The chief of police, who was present to see that everything was in order, put several questions to the purveyor, who told him the whole story of the death of the hunchback, and how he had carried the body to the place where it had been found by the Christian merchant.

'You are going,' he said to the chief of police, 'to kill an innocent man, for it is impossible that he should have murdered a creature who was dead already. It is bad enough for me to have slain a Mussulman without having it on my conscience that a Christian who is guiltless should suffer through my fault.'

Now the purveyor's speech had been made in a loud voice, and was heard by all the crowd, and even if he had wished it, the chief of police could not have escaped setting the merchant free.

'Loosen the cords from the Christian's neck,' he commanded, turning to the executioner, 'and hang this man in his place, seeing that by his own confession he is the murderer.'

The hangman did as he was bid, and was tying the cord firmly, when he was stopped by the voice of the neighbourhood doctor beseeching him to pause, for he had something very important to say. When he had fought his way through the crowd and reached the chief of police, 'Worshipful sir,' he began, 'this Mussulman whom you desire to hang is unworthy of death; I alone am guilty. Last night a man and a woman who were strangers to me knocked at my door, bringing with them a patient for me to cure. The servant opened it, but having no light was hardly able to make out their faces, though she readily agreed to wake me and to hand me the fee for my services. While she was telling me her story they seem to have carried the sick man to the top of the staircase and then left him there. I jumped up in a hurry without waiting for a lantern, and in the darkness I fell against something, which tumbled headlong down the stairs and never stopped till it reached the bottom. When I examined the body I found it was quite dead, and the corpse was that of a hunchback Mussulman. Terrified at what we had done, my wife and I took the body on the roof and let it down the chimney of our neighbour the purveyor, whom you were just about to hang. The purveyor, finding him in his room, naturally thought he was a thief, and struck him such a blow that the man fell down and lay motionless on the floor. Stooping to examine him, and finding him stone dead, the purveyor supposed that the man had died from the blow he had received; but of course this was a mistake, as you will see from my account, and I only am the murderer; and although I am innocent of any wish to commit a crime, I must suffer for it all the same, or else have the blood of two Mussulmen on my conscience. Therefore send away this man, I pray you, and let me take his place, as it is I who am guilty.'

On hearing the declaration of the neighbourhood doctor, the chief of police commanded that he should be led to the gallows, and the sultan's purveyor go free. The cord was placed around the neighbour's neck, and his feet had already ceased to touch the ground when the voice of the tailor was heard beseeching the executioner to pause one moment and to listen to what he had to say.

'Oh, my lord,' he cried, turning to the chief of police, 'how nearly have you caused the death of three innocent people! But if you will only have the patience to listen to my tale, you shall know who is the real culprit. If someone has to suffer, it must be me! Yesterday, at dusk, I was working in my shop with a light heart when the little hunchback, who was more than half drunk, came and sat in the doorway. He sang me several songs, and then I invited him to finish the evening at my house. He accepted my invitation, and we went away together. At supper I helped him to a slice of fish, but in eating it a bone stuck in his throat, and in spite of all we could do he died in a few minutes. We felt deeply sorry for his death, but fearing lest we should be held responsible, we carried the corpse to the house of the neighbourhood doctor. I knocked, and desired the servant to beg her master to come down as fast as possible and see a sick man whom we had brought for him to cure; and in order to hasten his movements I placed a piece of money in her hand as the doctor's fee. Directly she had disappeared I dragged the body to the top of the stairs, and then hurried away with my wife back to our house. In descending the stairs the doctor accidentally knocked over the corpse, and finding him dead believed that he himself was the murderer. But now you know the truth set him free, and let me die in his stead.'

The chief of police and the crowd of spectators were lost in astonishment at the strange events to which the death of the hunchback had given rise.

'Loosen the neighbourhood doctor,' said he to the hangman, 'and string up the tailor instead, since he has made confession of his crime. Really, one cannot deny that this is a very singular story, and it deserves to be written in letters of gold.'

The executioner speedily untied the knots which confined the doctor, and was passing the cord round the neck of the tailor, when the sultan of Kashgar, who had missed his jester, happened to make inquiry of his officers as to what had become of him.

'Sire,' replied they, 'the hunchback having drunk more than was good for him, escaped from the palace and was seen wandering about the town, where this morning he was found dead. A man was arrested for having caused his death, and held in custody till a gallows was erected. At the moment that he was about to suffer punishment, first one man arrived, and then another, each accusing themselves of the murder, and this went on for a long time, and at the present instant the chief of police is engaged in questioning a man who declares that he alone is the true assassin.'

The sultan of Kashgar no sooner heard these words than he ordered an usher to go to the chief of police and to bring all the persons concerned in the hunchback's death, together with the corpse, that he wished to see once again. The usher hastened on his errand, but was only just in time, for the tailor was positively swinging in the air, when his voice fell upon the silence of the crowd, commanding the hangman to cut down the body.

The hangman, recognizing the usher as one of the king's servants, cut down the tailor, and the usher, seeing the man was safe, sought the chief of police and gave him the sultan's message. Accordingly, the chief of police at once set out for the palace, taking with him the tailor, the doctor, the purveyor, and the merchant, who bore the dead hunchback on their shoulders.

When the procession reached the palace the chief of police prostrated himself at the feet of the sultan, and related all that he knew of the matter. The sultan was so much struck by the circumstances that he ordered his private historian to write down an exact account of what had passed, so that in the years to come the miraculous escape of the four men who had thought themselves murderers might never be forgotten.

The sultan asked everybody concerned in the hunchback's affair to tell him their stories. Among others was a prating barber, whose tale of one of his brothers follows.

From: The Arabian Nights Entertainments

The Bride of the Evil One

IN FORMER TIMES there lived, on a great plantation far out in the country, the richest and most beautiful lady in the world. Her name was Maritta, and she was beloved by all who knew her, especially so by her parents, with whom she dwelt.

She was so rich that one could not count her wealth in many days; and her home was a palace, filled with rare things from all quarters of the globe. Rich hangings of damask and tapestry adorned the walls, and massive and wonderfully carved furniture filled the rooms. Instead of gilt, as is usual in splendid mansions, the mirrors and pictures were framed in gold, silver, and even precious stones. Then, the dining table was a wonder to behold – glittering with costly glass and golden service. The lady Maritta always ate from a jewelled platter with a golden spoon; and her rooms were filled with wondrous vases, containing delicious spices and rare perfumes of many kinds.

Half the brave and daring fine gentlemen of her country had sought her hand in marriage; but her parents always declared that each was not rich enough. So loath were her parents to give her up, that they finally said she should never marry unless she could view her suitor ten thousand miles down the road.

Now, as roads in general are not straight for so great a distance, to say nothing of one's eyesight, the poor lady was quite in despair, and had almost decided to remain a spinster.

At last the Evil One, seeing the covetousness of this old couple, procured for himself an equipage of great magnificence, and went a-wooing. His coach was made of beaten gold, so ablaze with precious stones that the sun seemed mean in comparison with it. Maritta beheld it thirty thousand miles off, and all the household were called out to view it; for such a wonder had never been seen in that part of the world.

But so great was the Evil One's power for conjuring that he was a very short time in arriving. He drove up to the door with so grand a dash and clatter and style that Maritta thought she had never beheld as princely a personage. When he had alighted most gracefully, uncovering [removing his hat] and bowing to the mother and father, he knelt at the feet of Maritta, kissed her hand, and turning to her astonished parents, asked the hand of their daughter in marriage. So pleased were they all with his appearance that the wedding was hastened that very day.

After the marriage compact was completed Maritta bade adieu to her proud parents; and tripping lightly into his coach, they drove away with great effect.

Then they journeyed and journeyed, and every fine house or plantation which they approached, Maritta would exclaim, 'Is that your home, my dear?'

'No, darling,' he would reply with a knowing smile, 'my house is another cut to that.'

Still they journeyed: and just as Maritta was beginning to feel very weary they approached a great hill, from which was issuing a cloud of black smoke, and she could perceive an enormous hole in the side of the hill, which appeared like the entrance to a tunnel. The horses were now prancing and chafing at the bits in a most terrifying manner; and Maritta thought she saw flames coming from out their nostrils. just as she was catching her breath to ask the meaning of it all, the coach and party plunged suddenly into the mouth of the yawning crater, and they sank down, down into that place which is called Torment.

The poor trembling lady went into a swoon, and knew nothing more until she awoke in the House of Satan. But she did not yet know that it was the Evil One whom she had married, nor that, worse still, he was already a married man when she had made his acquaintance. Neither did she know that the frightful old crone was his other wife. Satan's manner had also undergone a decided change; and he, who had been so charming a lover, was now a blustering, insolent master. Lifting his voice until it shook the house, as when it thunders, he stormed around, beating the old hag, killing her uncanny black cat, and raising a tumult generally. Then, ordering the hag to cook him some buckwheat cakes for breakfast, he stamped out of the house, towards his blacksmith shop, to see how his hands were doing their work.

While the wretched young wife sat in her parlour, looking very mournful and lovely, wiping her eyes and feeling greatly mystified, the old hag was turning her cakes on the griddle and growing more and more jealous of this beautiful new wife who was to take her place. Finally she left the cakes and came and stood by Maritta.

'My child,' quoth she, 'my dear daughter, have you married that man?'

'Yes, dame,' replied the pretty Maritta.

'Well, my child,' said she, 'you have married nothing but the Devil.'

At this the wretched young wife uttered a scream and would have swooned again, except that the hag grasped her by the arm, and putting a rough horny hand over Maritta's mouth, said in a low and surly voice, near her ear, 'Hist! Should he hear you, he will kill us both! Only do my bidding, and keep a quiet tongue, and I will show you how to make your escape.'

At this Maritta sat up quite straight, and said in trembling tones, 'Good dame, prithee tell me, and I will obey, and when I am free, I will send you five millions of dollars.'

But the forlorn hag only shook her head, replying, 'Money I ask not, for it is of no use to such as I; but listen well.'

Then seating herself on the floor at the feet of Maritta, her black hair hanging in tangles about her sharp ugly face, like so many serpents, she continued in this wise, 'He has two roosters who are his spies, and you must give them a bushel of corn to pacify them – but I shall steal the corn for you. He also has two oxen; one is as swift of foot as the wind can blow; the other can only travel half as fast. You will have to choose the last, as the swift one is too well-guarded for us to reach him. The slower one is tethered just outside the door. Come!' she cried to Maritta, who would have held back, 'a faint heart will only dwell in Torment.'

At this thought the poor Maritta roused herself, and summoned all her strength. Her hair had now fallen loose and she was all in tears. But she mounted quickly, looking over her shoulder, to see if he was coming even then.

'But dame,' cried she, 'will he not overtake me, if his ox is so much more fleet of foot than mine?'

'Hold your slippery tongue,' replied the hag, 'and mark my words.

'Here is a drawstring bag to hang at your side; this is a brickbat which I put in the bottom, and on that I place a turkey egg and a goose egg. When you feel the hot steam coming near you, drop the brickbat – for he will soon return, and missing you, will start on your chase, mounted on the ox. As he approaches near, you will feel the heat of his breath like hot steam. When you drop the brickbat a wall will spring up from the earth to the sky; and the Devil cannot pass it until he tears down every brick, and throws it out of sight. When you feel the hot steam again, drop the turkey egg, and there will come a river; and when he reaches this river he cannot cross over until his ox drinks all the water. Do the same with the goose egg, and a river will again flow behind you, thus giving you more time in which to reach home. Now off with you, and Devil take you, if you don't hold on tight and keep up your spirits. But, hark ye, if he catches you, I will poison you when you come back.'

At this terrible threat the lovely Maritta was so frightened that she forgot to thank the old hag or say goodbye. In the twinkling of an eye the weird-looking creature had raised her mighty arm, and gurgling out a frightful laugh, she lashed the ox with a huge whip.

Away he sped, verily as fleet as the wind, with the beautiful lady clinging on, her arms wound around his neck, and her soft face buried in his shaggy hair. Onward they floated, above the earth, it seemed to Maritta, over hills and plains, through brake and swamp. Just as the lady began to rejoice at being set free, for it seemed a kind ox, and, after all, it was not so very hard to hold on, as she glided along, she heard a piercing shriek behind her; and suddenly a burning hot steam seemed to envelop her.

Thinking of the brickbat, in an instant she snatched it from the drawstring bag – almost breaking the eggs in her haste – and flung it behind her, nearly suffocated with the heat. Then she turned to look and lo! A great dark wall shut the awful sight from her gaze.

Onward, onward they sped, as she urged the ox by kind words, stroking his great neck with her delicate white hands. After they had traversed a great distance, Maritta began to think of home and her loved ones, when her reveries were broken by a gaunt black hand clutching at her hair over the back of the ox; and again she felt the intense heat. Too terrified to put her hand in the drawstring bag, she gave it a shake, and the turkey egg fell to the ground. On the instant water was flowing all about her, cooling the air and quite reviving her. Then a harsh voice fell upon her ear, crying, 'Drink, drink, I tell you; mighty hard on you, but you must drink!'

Soon the river was left far behind, and again Maritta aroused herself as she began to notice many familiar landmarks, which told that she was nearing home. After urging the ox on at a great rate for many more miles, she dropped the goose egg, in order to give herself ample time, although as yet she had not again felt the approach of her fiendish husband.

At length the welcome sight of her own broad fields greeted her anxious and weary eyes; and soon her dear home arose upon the horizon. With a few more strides the wonderful ox halted at her own very door, and she fell from his back more dead than alive. For some moments she was unable to rise and embrace her alarmed parents, who had seen her approach.

They had only had time to retire into the house, when Satan rode up to the steps. Throwing himself from the ox, he banged for admittance, in a vastly different manner from that of his first visit. But the father confronted him, and he had to content himself with talking to Maritta over her father's shoulders, while the poor lady was cowering in a corner of the room clinging to her mother. However, the touch of loving parental arms soon reassured her, and she demanded of Satan what he wished further.

'I have,' replied his Satanic majesty, 'three questions to propound to you; and if not properly answered, I shall take you by force again to my realms.'

Then placing his feet wide apart, with head thrown back, one arm akimbo on his hip, and snapping the fingers of his other hand, he sang in an impudent, swaggering manner:

'What is whiter than any snow?
What is whiter than any snow?
Who fell in the colley well?'

The gentle Maritta lifted her soft eyes, and raising her sweet voice sang in a pure and tender strain:

'Heaven is whiter than any snow,
Heaven is whiter than any snow,
Who fell in the colley well?'

'Yes, ma'am,' replied Satan, rather taken aback. 'That's right.'

Then he continued:

'What is deeper than any well,
What is deeper than any well,
Who fell in the colley well?'
Maritta replied in the same strain:
'Hell is deeper than any well,
Hell is deeper than any well,
Who fell in the colley well?'
Again the Evil One took up his strain:
'What is greener than any grass?
What is greener than any grass?
Who fell in the colley well?'
Maritta lifted her voice a third time:
'Poison is greener than any grass,
Poison is greener than any grass,
Who fell in the colley well?'

Greatly confounded at her answers, the Evil One stamped his feet in such a manner that smoke and sparks flew upward, and an odour of sulphur filled the room. Then turning on his heels he cried to the mother that he had left a note under the doorsteps with the Devil's own riddle on it.

A thousand or more acres of green corn grew about the house; and the Devil, pulling it all up by the roots, carried it in his hands, tore the roof off the mansion, and raising a fearful storm, disappeared in it.

When the storm had abated, the mountains around about were all levelled to the ground. After the panic caused by his wonderful conjuring had subsided, the mother bethought herself of the note, and when found it read as follows:

> Nine little white blocks into a pen,
> One little red block rolled over them.
> None could guess it save Maritta,
> Who said it meant the teeth and tongue.

From: English Folk-Tales in America

The Clever Thief

IN OLDEN TIMES there lived in a hill town a householder, who married a wife of his own caste.

When a son was born unto him, he said to his wife, 'Goodwife, now that there is born unto us a causer of debts and diminisher of means, I will take merchandise and go to sea.'

She replied, 'Do so, lord.'

So he went to sea with his merchandise, and there he died.

After his wife had got over her mourning, she continued to live, partly supported by her handiwork, and partly by her relatives.

Not far from her dwelt a weaver who was skilled in his art, and who by means of adroitness succeeded in everything. Seeing that he, by means of his art, had become well to do, she came to the conclusion that weaving was better than going to sea, for when a man did the latter, he needlessly exposed himself to misfortune.

So she said to the weaver, 'O brother, teach this nephew of yours to weave.'

He replied, 'As that is right, I will do so.'

The youth became his apprentice, and in a short time learnt the art of weaving, for he was sharp and quick.

As the weaver wore fine clothes, took good baths, and partook of delicate food, the youth said to him one day, 'Uncle, how is it that although you and I are occupied in exactly the same kind of work, yet you have fine clothes, good baths, and delicate food, but I never have a chance of such things?'

The weaver replied, 'Nephew, I carry on two kinds of work. By day I practise weaving, but by night thieving.'

'If that be so, uncle, I too will practise thieving.'

'Nephew, you cannot commit a theft.'

'Uncle, I can.'

The weaver thought he would test him a little, so he took him to the marketplace, purchased a hare there, and gave it to him, saying, 'Nephew, I shall take a bath and then return home. Meanwhile, go on roasting this hare.'

While he was taking his bath, the youth hastily roasted the hare and ate up one of its legs.

When the weaver returned from his bath, he said, 'Nephew, have you roasted the hare?'

'Yes!'

'Let's see it, then.'

When the youth had brought the hare, and the weaver saw that it only had three legs, he said, 'Nephew, where is the fourth leg gone?'

'Uncle, it is true that hares have four legs, but if the fourth leg is not there, it cannot have gone anywhere.'

The weaver thought, 'Although I have long been a thief, yet this lad is a still greater thief.'

And he went with the youth and the three-legged hare into a drinking house and called for liquor. When they had both drunk, the weaver said, 'Nephew, the score must be paid by a trick.'

'Uncle, he who has drunk may play a trick; why should I, who have not drunk, do this thing?'

The weaver saw that the lad was a great swindler, so he determined to carry out a theft along with him.

They betook themselves to housebreaking. Once when they had made a hole into a house, and the weaver was going to pass his head through the opening, the youth said, 'Uncle, although you are a thief, yet you do not understand your business. The legs should be put in first, not the head. For if the head should get cut off, its owner would be recognised, and his whole family would be plunged into ruin. Therefore put your feet in first.'

When the weaver had done so, attention was called to the fact, and a cry was raised of 'Thieves! Thieves!'

At that cry a great number of people assembled, who seized the weaver by his legs and began to pull him in. The youth, all by himself, could not succeed in pulling him out; but he cut off the weaver's head and got away with it.

The ministers brought the news to the king, saying, 'Your majesty, the thief was himself arrested at the spot where the housebreaking took place; but someone cut off his head and went away with it.'

The king said, 'O friends, he who has cut off the head and gone away with it is a great thief. Go and expose the headless trunk at the crossway of the main street. Then place yourselves on one side, and arrest whoever embraces it and wails over it, for that will be the thief.'

Thereupon those servants of the king exposed the headless trunk at the crossway of the main street, and stationed themselves on one side.

Thinking it would be wrong not to embrace his uncle and moan over him, the other thief assumed the appearance of a madman, and took to embracing men, women, carts, horses, bullocks, buffaloes, goats, and dogs.

Afterwards, all men thinking he was mad, he pressed the headless trunk to his breast, wailed over it as long as he liked, and then went his way. The king was informed by his men that a madman had pressed the headless trunk to his bosom, and while he held it there had wailed over it, and had then gone away.

The king said, 'O friends, this man of a surety was the other thief. Ye have acted wrongly in not laying hands upon him. Therefore shall hands be laid upon you.'

The other thief said to himself, 'If I do not show honour to my uncle, I shall be acting badly.'

So he assumed the appearance of a carter, and drove a cart up to the spot laden with dry wood. When he arrived there, he upset the cart with its load of dry wood, unyoked the oxen, set the cart on fire, and then went away. The headless trunk was consumed by the flames.

The king was informed by his men that the corpse was burnt, and they told him all that had taken place. The king said, 'O friends, the carter was certainly the thief. Ye have acted wrongly in not laying hands upon him. Therefore shall hands be laid upon you.'

The thief said to himself, 'I shall not be acting rightly unless I take soul offerings to the burial place for my uncle.'

So he assumed the appearance of a Brahman, and wandered from house to house collecting food. From what he collected he made five oblation cakes, which he left at the burial place, and then went his way. The king's men told him that a Brahman had wandered from house to house collecting food, and had then left five oblation cakes on the spot where the body had been burnt, and had then gone away.

The king said, 'O friends, that was really the thief. Ye have acted wrongly in not laying hands upon him.'

The thief thought, 'I shall be acting badly if I do not throw my uncle's bones into the Ganges.'

So he assumed the appearance of a Kāpālika, went to the place where the corpse had been burnt, smeared his body with ashes, filled a skull with bones and ashes, flung it into the Ganges, and then went his way. When the king had been told by his men all that had happened, he said, 'O friends, this was really the thief. Ye have acted wrongly in not laying hands upon him. In order to bring the matter to an end, do ye let it alone. I will lay hands on the man myself.'

The king had a garden laid out at a spot where the Ganges formed a bay, and he set men to watch on both of its shores. In it he stationed his very beautiful daughter on the shore of the river, giving her orders to cry aloud in case anyone tried to touch her. To the watchmen also he gave orders to repair to the park as soon as they heard any sound, and if any man was found there, to seize him and bring him before him. Now the thief thought that he must not allow the opportunity of enjoying the king's daughter to slip out of his hands.

So he took an empty pitcher, went down to the shore of the Ganges, and began to draw water. As he was carrying the first pitcherful, the watchmen came running up, thinking that he was the thief, and hit him a blow, in consequence of which the pitcher was broken. As he was carrying the second pitcherful, his pitcher was broken in the same way. But after this had happened three times, the watchmen came to the conclusion that he was a water carrier, and paid him no more attention. Then the thief covered his head with a pot, and swam down the stream to the bay.

There he came ashore and said to the maiden, 'If you utter a single cry you shall die.' In her fright she remained silent. He tarried awhile with her, and then went his way. The watchmen did not know what to do, seeing that she had made no noise while the thief tarried with her, and had not begun to cry till he had satisfied himself and gone away; but they gave the king a full account of what had taken place.

The king said, 'It is a bad business that he was not caught.'

The result of the thief's visit was that, after eight or nine months had elapsed, the princess bore a son. When the thief heard of this, he decided that he must not miss his son's birth feast, so he assumed the appearance of a courtier and betook himself to the king's palace. As he was leaving the palace he called out to the royal servants, 'O friends, by order of the king, plunder the merchants' quarter!'

As the servants thought that the king had given permission for the plundering of the merchants' quarter in honour of his grandson's birth, they set to work thereat. In consequence of this a great outcry arose, and the king asked what was the meaning of it.

When the ministers had supplied him with a full account, the king said, 'If this be so, I also have been taken

61

in by him. Wherefore, if I do not punish him, I shall lose my throne.'

With this idea in view he caused an enclosure to be made, and, after some little time had elapsed, he ordered his ministers to make public through the realm a proclamation to the effect that all men who dwelt in the kingdom were bound to assemble within that enclosure; and that no excuse would avail, but if anyone did not appear he should be punished.

When the ministers had made this order public, and all the inhabitants of the realm were assembled together, the king gave the boy a wreath of flowers, and told him to give it to the man who was his father; and he gave orders to the watchmen to lay hands upon the man to whom the boy should give the wreath.

As the boy walked with the wreath through the assembled crowds and closely observed them, he caught sight of the thief, and, in accordance with the incomprehensible sequence of human affairs, handed him the wreath. The king's watchmen seized the thief and brought him before the king.

The king asked his ministers what ought to be done. They were of opinion that the thief must be put to death.

But the king said, 'O friends, so little does such a hero of a man deserve to be put to death, that he ought much rather to be carefully watched over.'

Thereupon he endowed his daughter with ornaments of all sorts, and gave her to the thief as his wife, and bestowed upon her the half of his kingdom.

From: Tibetan Tales

The Swallow King's Rewards

In the province of Chullado, in Southern Korea, lived two brothers.

One was very rich, the other very poor. For in dividing the inheritance, the elder brother, instead of taking the father's place, and providing for the younger children, kept the whole property to himself, allowing his younger brother nothing at all, and reducing him to a condition of abject misery.

Both men were married. Nahl Bo, the elder, had many concubines, in addition to his wife, but had no children; while Hyung Bo had but one wife and several children. The former's wives were continually quarrelling; the latter lived in contentment and peace with his wife, each endeavouring to help the other bear the heavy burdens circumstances had placed upon them.

The elder brother lived in a fine, large compound, with warm, comfortable houses; the younger had built himself a hut of broom straw, the thatch of which was so poor that when it rained they were deluged inside, upon the earthen floor. The room was so small, too, that when Hyung Bo stretched out his legs in his sleep his feet were apt to be thrust through the wall. They had no *kang*, and had to sleep upon the cold dirt floor, where insects were so abundant as to often succeed in driving the sleepers out of doors.

They had no money for the comforts of life, and were glad when a stroke of good fortune enabled them to obtain the necessities. Hyung Bo worked whenever he could get work, but rainy days and dull seasons were a heavy strain upon them.

The wife did plain sewing, and together they made straw sandals for the peasants and vendors. At fair time, the sandal business was good, but then came a time when no more food was left in the house, the string for making the sandals was all used up, and they had no money for a new supply.

Then the children cried to their mother for food, till her heart ached for them, and the father wandered off in a last attempt to get something to keep the breath of life in his family.

Not a kernel of rice was left.

A poor rat which had cast in his lot with this kind family became desperate when, night after night, he chased around the little house without being able to find the semblance of a meal. Becoming desperate, he vented his despair in such loud squealing that he wakened the neighbours, who declared that the mouse said his legs were worn off running about in a vain search for a grain of rice with which to appease his hunger. The famine became so serious in the little home, that at last the mother commanded her son to go to his uncle and tell him plainly how distressed they were, and ask him to loan them enough rice to subsist on till they could get work, when they would surely return the loan.

The boy did not want to go.

His uncle would never recognize him on the street, and he was afraid to go inside his house lest he should whip him. But the mother commanded him to go, and he obeyed. Outside his uncle's house were many cows, well-fed and valuable. In pens, he saw great fat pigs in abundance, and fowls were everywhere in great numbers.

Many dogs also were there, and they ran barking at him, tearing his clothes with their teeth and frightening him so much that he was tempted to run; but speaking kindly to them, they quieted down, and one dog came and licked his hand as if ashamed of the conduct of the others.

A female servant ordered him away, but he told her he was her master's nephew, and wanted to see him; whereupon she smiled but let him pass into an inner court, where he found his uncle sitting on the little veranda under the broad, overhanging eaves.

The man gruffly demanded, 'Who are you?'

'I am your brother's son,' he said. 'We are starving at our house, and have had no food for three days. My father is away now trying to find work, but we are very hungry, and only ask you to loan us a little rice till we can get some to return you.'

The uncle's eyes drew down to a point, his brows contracted, and he seemed very angry, so that the nephew began looking for an easy way of escape in case he should come at him. At last he looked up and said: 'My rice is locked up, and I have ordered the granaries not to be opened. The flour is sealed and cannot be broken into. If I give you some cold victuals, the dogs will bark at you and try to take it from you. If I give you the leavings of the wine press, the pigs will be jealous and squeal at you. If I give you bran, the cows and fowls will take after you. Get out, and let me never see you here again.'

So saying, he caught the poor boy by the collar and threw him into the outer court, hurting him, and causing him to cry bitterly with pain of body and distress of mind.

At home the poor mother sat jogging her babe in her weak arms, and appeasing the other children by saying that brother had gone to their uncle for food, and soon the pot would be boiling and they would all be satisfied. When, hearing a footfall, all scrambled eagerly to the door, only to see the empty-handed, red-eyed boy coming along, trying manfully to look cheerful.

'Did your uncle whip you?' asked the mother, more eager for the safety of her son, than to have her own crying want allayed.

'No,' stammered the brave boy.

'He had gone to the capital on business,' said he, hoping to thus prevent further questioning, on so troublesome a subject.

'What shall I do?' queried the poor woman, amidst the crying and moaning of her children.

There was nothing to do but starve, it seemed. However, she thought of her own straw shoes, which were scarcely used, and these she sent to the market, where they brought three *cash*. This pittance was invested equally in rice, beans, and vegetables; eating which they were relieved for the present, and with full stomachs the little ones fell to playing happily once more, but the poor mother was full of anxiety for the morrow.

Their fortune had turned, however, with their new lease of life, for the father returned with a bale of faggots he had gathered on the mountains, and with the proceeds of these the shoes were redeemed and more food was purchased. Bright and early then next morning both parents went forth in search of work. The wife secured employment winnowing rice.

The husband overtook a boy bearing a pack, but his back was so blistered, he could with difficulty carry his burden. Hyung Bo adjusted the saddle of the pack frame to his own back, and carried it for the boy, who, at their arrival at his destination in the evening, gave his helper some cash, in addition to his lodging and meals.

During the night, however, a gentleman wished to send a letter by rapid dispatch to a distant place, and Hyung Bo was paid well for carrying it.

Returning from this profitable errand, he heard of a very rich man, who had been seized by the corrupt local magistrate, on a false accusation, and was to be beaten publicly, unless he consented to pay a heavy sum as hush money.

Hearing of this, Hyung went to see the rich prisoner, and arranged with him that he would act as his substitute for three thousand *cash*. The man was very glad to get off so easily, and Hyung took the beating. He limped to his house, where his poor wife greeted him with tears and lamentations, for he was a sore and sorry sight indeed.

He was cheerful, however, for he explained to them that this had been a rich day's work; he had simply submitted to a little whipping, and was to get three thousand *cash* for it.

The money did not come, however, for the fraud was detected, and the original prisoner was also punished. Being of rather a close disposition, the man seemed to think it unnecessary to pay for what did him no good.

Then the wife cried indeed over her husband's wrongs and their own more unfortunate condition. But the husband cheered her, saying: 'If we do right we will surely succeed.'

He was right. Spring was coming on, and he soon got work at ploughing and sowing seed. They gave their little house the usual spring cleaning, and decorated the door with appropriate legends, calling upon the fates to bless with prosperity the little home.

With the spring came the birds from the south country, and they seemed to have a preference for the home of this poor family – as indeed did the rats and insects. The birds built their nests under the eaves. They were swallows, and as they made their little mud air castles, Hyung Bo said to his wife: 'I am afraid to have these birds build their nests there. Our house is so weak it may fall down, and then what will the poor birds do?'

But the little visitors seemed not alarmed, and remained with the kind people, apparently feeling safe under the friendly roof.

By and by the little nests were full of commotion and bluster; the eggs had opened, and circles of wide-opened mouths could be seen in every nest. Hyung and his children were greatly interested in this new addition to their family circle, and often gave them bits of their own scanty allowance of food, so that the birds became quite tame and hopped in and out of the hut at will.

One day, when the little birds were taking their first lesson in flying, Hyung was lying on his back on the ground, and saw a huge roof snake crawl along and devour several little birds before he could arise and help them. One bird struggled from the reptile and fell, but, catching both legs in the fine meshes of a reed-blind, they were broken, and the little fellow hung helplessly within the snake's reach.

Hyung hastily snatched it down, and with the help of his wife he bound up the broken limbs, using dried fish skin for splints. He laid the little patient in a warm place, and the bones speedily united, so that the bird soon began to hop around the room, and pick up bits of food laid out for him. Soon the splints were removed, however, and he flew away, happily, to join his fellows.

The autumn came; and one evening – it was the ninth day of the ninth moon – as the little family were sitting about the door, they noticed the bird with the crooked legs sitting on the clothesline and singing to them.

'I believe he is thanking us and saying goodbye,' said Hyung, 'for the birds are all going south now.'

That seemed to be the truth, for they saw their little friend no longer, and they felt lonely without the occupants of the now deserted nests. The birds, however, were paying homage to the king of birds in the bird-land beyond the frosts. And as the king saw the little crooked-legged bird come along, he demanded an explanation of the strange sight.

Thereupon the little fellow related his narrow escape from a snake that had already devoured many of his brothers and cousins, the accident in the blind, and his rescue and subsequent treatment by a very poor but very kind man.

His bird majesty was very much entertained and pleased. He thereupon gave the little cripple a seed engraved with fine characters in gold, denoting that the seed belonged to the gourd family. This seed the bird was to give to his benefactor in the spring.

The winter wore away, and the spring found the little family almost as destitute as when first we described them. One day they heard a familiar bird song, and, running out, they saw their little crooked-legged friend with something in its mouth, that looked like a seed. Dropping its burden to the ground, the little bird sang to them of the king's gratitude, and of the present he had sent, and then flew away.

Hyung picked up the seed with curiosity, and on one side he saw the name of its kind, on the other, in fine gold characters, was a message saying: 'Bury me in soft earth, and give me plenty of water.'

They did so, and in four days the little shoot appeared in the fine earth. They watched its remarkable growth with eager interest as the stem shot up, and climbed all over the house, covering it up as a bower, and threatening to break down the frail structure with the added weight. It blossomed, and soon four small gourds began to form. They grew to an enormous size, and Hyung could scarcely keep from cutting them.

His wife prevailed on him to wait till the frost had made them ripe, however, as then they could cut them, eat the inside, and make water vessels of the shells, which they could then sell, and thus make a double profit. He waited, though with a poor grace, till the ninth moon, when the gourds were left alone, high upon the roof, with only a trace of the shrivelled stems which had planted them there.

Hyung got a saw and sawed open the first huge gourd. He worked so long, that when his task was finished he feared he must be in a swoon, for out of the opened gourd stepped two beautiful boys, with fine bottles of wine and a table of jade set with dainty cups. Hyung staggered back and sought assurance of his wife, who was fully as dazed, as was her husband.

The surprise was somewhat relieved by one of the handsome youths stepping forth, placing the table before them, and announcing that the bird king had sent them with these presents to the benefactor of one of his subjects – the bird with broken legs. Ere they could answer, the other youth placed a silver bottle on the table, saying: 'This wine will restore life to the dead.'

Another, which he placed on the table, would, he said, restore sight to the blind.

Then going to the gourd, he brought two gold bottles: one contained a tobacco, which, being smoked, would give speech to the dumb, while the other gold bottle contained wine which would prevent the approach of age and ward off death.

Having made these announcements, the pair disappeared, leaving Hyung and his wife almost dumb with amazement. They looked at the gourd, then at the little table and its contents, and each looked at the other to be sure it was not a dream. At length Hyung broke the silence, remarking that, as he was very hungry, he would venture to open another gourd, in the hope that it would be found full of something good to eat, since it was not so important for him to have something with which to restore life just now as it was to have something to sustain life with.

The next gourd was opened as was the first, when by some means out flowed all manner of household furniture, and clothing, with rolls upon rolls of fine silk and satin cloth, linen goods, and the finest cotton. The satin alone was far greater in bulk than the gourd had been, yet, in addition, the premises were literally strewn with costly furniture and the finest fabrics. They barely examined the goods now, their amazement having become so great that they could scarcely wait until all had been opened, and the whole seemed so unreal, that they feared delay might be dangerous.

Both sawed away on the next gourd, when out came a body of carpenters, all equipped with tools and lumber, and, to their utter and complete amazement, began putting up a house as quickly and quietly as thought, so that before they could arise from the ground they saw a fine house standing before them, with courts and servants' quarters, stables, and granaries. Simultaneously a great train of bulls and ponies appeared, loaded down with rice and other products as tributes from the district in which the place was located. Others came bringing money tribute, servants – male and female – and clothing.

They felt sure they were in dreamland now, and that they might enjoy the exercise of power while it lasted, they began commanding the servants to put the goods away, the money in the *sahrang*, or reception room, the clothing in the *tarack*, or garret over the fireplace, the rice in the granaries, and animals in their stables. Others were sent to prepare a bath, that they might don the fine clothing before it should be too late. The servants obeyed, increasing the astonishment of the pair, and causing them to literally forget the fourth gourd in their amazed contemplation of the wondrous miracles being performed, and the dreamy air of satisfaction and contentment with which it surrounded them.

Their attention was called to the gourd by the servants, who were then commanded to carefully saw it open. They did so, and out stepped a maiden, as beautiful as were the gifts that had preceded her. Never before had Hyung looked on anyone who could at all compare with the matchless beauty and grace of the lovely creature who now stood so modestly and confidingly before him. He could find no words to express his boundless admiration, and could only stand in mute wonder and feast himself upon her beauty. Not so with his wife, however. She saw only a rival in the beautiful girl, and straightway demanded who she was, whence she came, and what she wanted. The maid replied: 'I am sent by the bird king to be this man's concubine.'

Whereupon the wife grew dark in the face, and ordered her to go whence she came and not see her husband again. She upbraided him for not being content with a house and estate, numbers of retainers and quantities of money, and declared this last trouble was all due to his greed in opening the fourth gourd.

Her husband had by this time found his speech, however, and severely reprimanded her for conducting herself in such a manner upon the receipt of such heavenly gifts, while yesterday she had been little more than a beggar; he commanded her to go at once to the women's quarters, where she should reign supreme, and never make such a display of her ill-temper again, under penalty of being consigned to a house by herself. The maiden he gladly welcomed, and conducted her to apartments set aside for her.

When Nahl Bo heard of the wonderful change taking place at his brother's establishment, he went himself to look into the matter. He found the report not exaggerated, and began to upbraid his brother with dishonest methods, which accusation the brother stoutly denied, and further demanded where, and of whom, he could steal a house, such rich garments, fine furniture, and have it removed in a day to the site of his former hovel.

Nahl Bo demanded an explanation, and Hyung Bo frankly told him how he had saved the bird from the snake and had bound up its broken limbs, so that it recovered; how the bird in return brought him a seed engraved with gold characters, instructing him how to plant and rear it; and how, having done so, the four gourds were born on the stalk, and from them, on ripening, had appeared these rich gifts.

The ill-favoured brother even then persisted in his charges, and in a gruff, ugly manner accused Hyung Bo of being worse than a thief in keeping all these fine goods, instead of dutifully sharing them with his elder brother. This insinuation of undutiful conduct really annoyed Hyung Bo, who, in his kindness of heart, forgave this unbrotherly senior his former ill conduct, and thinking only of his own present good fortune, he kindly bestowed considerable gifts upon the undeserving brother, and doubtless would have done more but that the covetous man espied the fair maiden, and at once insisted on having her. This was too much even for the patient Hyung Bo, who refused with a determination remarkable for him. A quarrel ensued, during which the elder brother took his departure in a rage, fully determined to use the secret of his brother's success for all it was worth in securing rich gifts for himself.

Going home he struck at all the birds he could see, and ordered his servants to do the same. After killing many, he succeeded in catching one, and, breaking its legs, he took fish skin and bound them up in splints, laying the little sufferer in a warm place, till it recovered and flew away, bandages and all. The result was as expected. The bird being questioned by the bird king concerning its crooked legs, related its story, dwelling, however, on the man's cruelty in killing so many birds and then breaking its own legs. The king understood thoroughly, and gave the little cripple a seed to present to the wicked man on its return in the spring.

Springtime came, and one day, as Nahl Bo was sitting cross-legged in the little room opening on the veranda off his court, he heard a familiar birdsong. Dropping his long pipe, he threw open the paper windows, and there, sure enough, sat a crooked-legged bird on the clothesline, bearing a seed in its mouth. Nahl Bo would let no one touch it, but as the bird dropped the seed and flew away, he jumped out so eagerly that he forgot to slip his shoes on, and got his clean white stockings all befouled. He secured the seed, however, and felt that his fortune was made. He planted it carefully, as directed, and gave it his personal attention.

The vines were most luxurious. They grew with great rapidity, till they had well nigh covered the whole of his large house and outbuildings.

Instead of one gourd, or even four, as in the brother's case, the new vines bore twelve gourds, which grew and grew till the great beams of his house fairly groaned under their weight, and he had to block them in place to keep them from rolling off the roofs. He had to hire men to guard them carefully, for now that the source of Hyung Bo's riches was understood, everyone was anxious for a gourd. They did not know the secret, however, which Nahl Bo concealed through selfishness, and Hyung through fear that everyone would take to killing and maiming birds as his wicked brother had done.

Maintaining a guard was expensive, and the plant so loosened the roof tiles, by the tendrils searching for earth and moisture in the great layer of clay under the tiles, that the rainy season made great havoc with his house. Large portions of plaster from the inside fell upon the paper ceilings, which in turn gave way, letting the dirty water drip into the rooms, and making the house almost uninhabitable.

At last, however, the plants could do no more harm; the frost had come, the vines had shrivelled away, and the enormous ripe gourds were carefully lowered, amid the yelling of a score of coolies, as each seemed to get in the others' way trying to manipulate the ropes and poles with which the gourds were let down to the ground. Once inside the court, and the great doors locked, Nahl Bo felt relieved, and shutting out everyone but a carpenter and his assistant, he prepared for the great surprise which he knew must await him, in spite of his most vivid dreams.

The carpenter insisted upon the enormous sum of a thousand cash for opening each gourd, and as he was too impatient to await the arrival of another, and as he expected to be of princely wealth in a few moments, Nahl Bo agreed to the exorbitant price.

Whereupon, carefully bracing a gourd, the men began sawing it through. It seemed a long time before the gourd fell in halves. When it did, out came a party of rope dancers, such as perform at fairs and public places. Nahl Bo was unprepared for any such surprise as this, and fancied it must be some great mistake. They sang and danced about as well as the crowded condition of the court would allow, and the family looked on complacently, supposing that the band had been sent to celebrate their coming good fortune.

But Nahl Bo soon had enough of this. He wanted to get at his riches, and seeing that the actors were about to stretch their ropes for a more extensive performance, he ordered them to cease and take their departure. To his amazement, however, they refused to do this, until he had paid them five thousand cash for their trouble.

'You sent for us and we came,' said the leader. 'Now pay us, or we will live with you till you do.'

There was no help for it, and with great reluctance and some foreboding, he gave them the money and dismissed them. Then Nahl Bo turned to the carpenter, who chanced to be a man with an ugly visage, made uglier by a great harelip.

'You,' he said, 'are the cause of all this. Before you entered this court these gourds were filled with gold, and your ugly face has changed it to beggars.'

Number two was opened with no better results, for out came a body of Buddhist priests, begging for their temple, and promising many sons in return for offerings of suitable merit. Although disgusted beyond measure, Nahl Bo still had faith in the gourds, and to get rid of the priests, lest they should see his riches, he gave them also five thousand cash.

As soon as the priests were gone, gourd number three was opened, with still poorer results, for out came a procession of paid mourners followed by a corpse borne by bearers. The mourners wept as loudly as possible, and all was in a perfect uproar. When ordered to go, the mourners declared they must have money for mourning, and to pay for burying the body.

Seeing no possible help for it, five thousand cash was finally given them, and they went out with the bier. Then Nahl Bo's wife came into the court, and began to abuse the hare-lipped man for bringing upon them all this trouble. Whereupon the latter became angry and demanded his money that he might leave. They had no intention of giving up the search as yet, however, and, as it was too late to change carpenters, the ugly fellow was paid for the work already done, and given an advance on that yet remaining. He therefore set to work upon the fourth gourd, which Nahl Bo watched with feverish anxiety.

From this one there came a band of *gee sang*, or dancing girls. There was one woman from each province, and each had her song and dance. One sang of the *yang wang*, or wind god; another of the *wang jay*, or pan deity; one sang of the *sung jee*, or money that is placed as a christening on the roof-tree of every house. There was the cuckoo song. The song of the ancient tree that has lived so long that its heart is dead and gone, leaving but a hollow space, yet the leaves spring forth every springtide.

The song of laughter and mourning, with an injunction to see to it that the rice offering be made to the departed spirits. To the king of the sun and stars a song was sung.

And last of all, one votary sang of the twelve months that make the year, the twelve hours that make the day, the thirty days that make the month, and of the new year's birth, as the old year dies, taking with it their ills to be buried in the past, and reminding all people to celebrate the New Year holidays by donning clean clothes and feasting on good food, that the following year may be to them one of plenty and prosperity.

Having finished their songs and their graceful posturing and waving of their gay silk banners, the *gee sang* demanded their pay, which had to be given them, reducing the family wealth five thousand cash more.

The wife now tried to persuade Nahl Bo to stop and not open more, but the harelip man offered to open the next for five hundred cash, as he was secretly enjoying the sport. So the fifth was opened a little, when a yellow-looking substance was seen inside, which was taken to be gold, and they hurriedly opened it completely.

But instead of gold, out came an acrobatic pair, being a strong man with a youth dressed to represent a girl. The man danced about, holding his young companion balanced upon his shoulders, singing meanwhile a song of an ancient king, whose riotous living was so distasteful to his subjects that he built him a cavernous palace, the floor of which was covered with quicksilver, the walls were decorated with jewels, and myriad lamps turned the darkness into day. Here were to be found the choicest viands and wines, with bands of music to entertain the feasters: most beautiful women; and he enjoyed himself most luxuriously until his enemy, learning the secret, threw open the cavern to the light of day, when all of the beautiful women immediately disappeared in the sun's rays.

Before he could get these people to discontinue their performance, Nahl Bo had to give them also five thousand cash. Yet in spite of all his ill luck, he decided to open another. Which being done, a jester came forth, demanding the expense money for his long journey. This was finally given him, for Nahl Bo had hit upon what he deemed a clever expedient. He took the wise fool aside, and asked him to use his wisdom in pointing out to him which of these gourds contained gold. Whereupon the jester looked wise, tapped several gourds, and motioned to each one as being filled with gold.

The seventh was therefore opened, and a lot of yamen runners came forth, followed by an official. Nahl Bo tried to run from what he knew must mean an exorbitant 'squeeze,' but he was caught and beaten for his indiscretion. The official called for his valise, and took from it a paper, which his secretary read, announcing that Nahl Bo was the serf of this lord and must hereafter pay to him a heavy tribute.

At this they groaned in their hearts, and the wife declared that even now the money was all gone, even to the last cash, while the rabble which had collected had stolen nearly everything worth removing. Yet the officer's servants demanded pay for their services, and they had to be given a note secured on the property before they would leave. Matters were now so serious that they could not be made much worse, and it was decided to open each remaining gourd, that if there were any gold they might have it.

When the next one was opened a bevy of *moo tang* women (soothsayers) came forth, offering to drive away the spirit of disease and restore the sick to health. They arranged their banners for their usual dancing ceremony, brought forth their drums, with which to exorcise the demons, and called for rice to offer to the spirits and clothes to burn for the spirits' apparel.

'Get out!' roared Nahl Bo. 'I am not sick except for the visitation of such as yourselves, who are forever burdening the poor, and demanding pay for your supposed services. Away with you, and befool some other *pah sak ye* (eight month's man – fool) if you can. I want none of your services.'

They were no easier to drive away, however, than were the other annoying visitors that had come with his supposed good fortune. He had finally to pay them as he had the others; and dejectedly he sat, scarcely noticing the opening of the ninth gourd.

The latter proved to contain a juggler, and the exasperated Nahl Bo, seeing but one small man, determined to make short work of him.

Seizing him by his topknot of hair, he was about to drag him to the door, when the dexterous fellow, catching his tormentor by the thighs, threw him headlong over his own back, nearly breaking his neck, and causing him to lie stunned for a time, while the expert bound him hand and foot, and stood him on his head, so that the wife was glad to pay the fellow and dismiss him ere the life should be departed from her lord.

On opening the tenth a party of blind men came out, picking their way with their long sticks, while their sightless orbs were raised towards the unseen heavens. They offered to tell the fortunes of the family. But, while their services might have been demanded earlier, the case was now too desperate for any such help.

The old men tinkled their little bells, and chanted some poetry addressed to the four good spirits stationed at the four corners of the earth, where they patiently stand bearing the world upon their shoulders; and to the distant heavens that arch over and fold the earth in their embrace, where the two meet at the far horizon (as pictured in the Korean flag). The blind men threw their dice, and, fearing lest they should prophesy death, Nahl Bo quickly paid and dismissed them.

The next gourd was opened but a trifle, that they might first determine as to the wisdom of letting out its contents. Before they could determine, however, a voice like thunder was heard from within, and the huge form of a giant arose, splitting open the gourd as he came forth. In his anger he seized poor Nahl Bo and tossed him upon his shoulders as though he would carry him away.

Whereupon the wife plead with tears for his release, and gladly gave an order for the amount of the ransom. After which the monster allowed the frightened man to fall to the ground, nearly breaking his aching bones in the fall.

The carpenter did not relish the sport any longer; it seemed to be getting entirely too dangerous. He thereupon demanded the balance of his pay, which they finally agreed to give him, providing he would open the last remaining gourd. For the desperate people hoped to find this at least in sufficient condition that they might cook or make soup of it, since they had no food left at all and no money, while the other gourds were so spoiled by the tramping of the feet of their unbidden guests, as to be totally unfit for food.

The man did as requested, but had only sawed a very little when the gourd split open as though it were rotten, while a most awful stench arose, driving everyone from the premises. This was followed by a gale of wind, so severe as to destroy the buildings, which, in falling, took fire from the *kang*, and while the once prosperous man looked on in helpless misery, the last of his remaining property was swept forever from him.

The seed that had brought prosperity to his honest, deserving brother had turned prosperity into ruin to the cruel, covetous Nahl Bo, who now had to subsist upon the charity of his kind brother, whom he had formerly treated so cruelly.

From: Korean Tales

The Myddvai Legend

A WIDOW, WHO had an only son, was obliged, in consequence of the large flocks she possessed, to send, under the care of her son, a portion of her cattle to graze on the Black Mountain near a small lake called Llyn-y-Van-Bach.

One day the son perceived, to his great astonishment, a most beautiful creature with flowing hair sitting on the unruffled surface of the lake combing her tresses, the water serving as a mirror. Suddenly she beheld the young man standing on the brink of the lake with his eyes rivetted on her, and unconsciously offering to herself the provision of barley bread and cheese with which he had been provided when he left his home.

Bewildered by a feeling of love and admiration for the object before him, he continued to hold out his hand towards the lady, who imperceptibly glided near to him, but gently refused the offer of his provisions. He attempted to touch her, but she eluded his grasp, saying:

'Cras dy fara;
Nid hawdd fy nala.

Hard baked is thy bread;
It is not easy to catch me.'

She immediately dived under the water and disappeared, leaving the love-stricken youth to return home, a prey to disappointment and regret that he had been unable to make further acquaintance with the lovely maiden with whom he had desperately fallen in love.

On his return home, he communicated to his mother the extraordinary vision. She advised him to take some unbaked dough the next time in his pocket, as there must have been some spell connected with the hard baked bread, or 'Bara Cras,' which prevented his catching the lady.

Next morning, before the sun was up, the young man was at the lake, not for the purpose of looking after the cattle, but that he might again witness the enchanting vision of the previous day. In vain did he glance over the surface of the lake; nothing met his view, save the ripples occasioned by a stiff breeze, and a dark cloud hung heavily on the summit of the Van.

Hours passed on, the wind was hushed, the overhanging clouds had vanished, when the youth was startled by seeing some of his mother's cattle on the precipitous side of the acclivity, nearly on the opposite side of the lake. As he was hastening away to rescue them from their perilous position, the object of his search again appeared to him, and seemed much more beautiful than when he first beheld her. His hand was again held out to her, full of unbaked bread, which he offered to her with an urgent proffer of his heart also, and vows of eternal attachment, all of which were refused by her, saying,

> 'Llaith dy fara!
> Ti ni fynna.
> Unbaked is thy bread!
> I will not have thee.'

But the smiles that played upon her features as the lady vanished beneath the waters forbade him to despair, and cheered him on his way home. His aged parent was acquainted with his ill success, and she suggested that his bread should the next time be but slightly baked, as most likely to please the mysterious being.

Impelled by love, the youth left his mother's home early next morning. He was soon near the margin of the lake impatiently awaiting the reappearance of the lady. The sheep and goats browsed on the precipitous sides of the Van, the cattle strayed amongst the rocks, rain and sunshine came and passed away, unheeded by the youth who was wrapped up in looking for the appearance of her who had stolen his heart. The sun was verging towards the west, and the young man casting a sad look over the waters ere departing homewards was astonished to see several cows walking along its surface, and, what was more pleasing to his sight, the maiden reappeared, even lovelier than ever.

She approached the land and he rushed to meet her in the water. A smile encouraged him to seize her hand, and she accepted the moderately baked bread he offered her, and after some persuasion she consented to become his wife, on condition that they should live together until she received from him three blows without a cause, 'Tri ergyd diachos' – Three causeless blows – when, should he ever happen to strike her three such blows, she would leave him forever.

These conditions were readily and joyfully accepted.

Thus the Lady of the Lake became engaged to the young man, and having loosed her hand for a moment she darted away and dived into the lake. The grief of the lover at this disappearance of his affianced was such that he determined to cast himself headlong into its unfathomed depths, and thus end his life.

As he was on the point of committing this rash act, there emerged out of the lake two most beautiful ladies, accompanied by a hoary-headed man of noble mien and extraordinary stature, but having otherwise all the force and strength of youth. This man addressed the youth, saying that, as he proposed to marry one of his daughters, he consented to the union, provided the young man could distinguish which of the two ladies before him was the object of his affections. This was no easy task, as the maidens were perfect counterparts of each other.

Whilst the young man narrowly scanned the two ladies and failed to perceive the least difference betwixt the two, one of them thrust her foot a slight degree forward. The motion, simple as it was, did not escape the observation of the youth, and he discovered a trifling variation in the mode in which their sandals were tied. This at once put an end to the dilemma, for he had on previous occasions noticed the peculiarity of her shoe tie, and he boldly took hold of her hand.

'Thou hast chosen rightly,' said the Father, 'be to her a kind and faithful husband, and I will give her, as a dowry, as many sheep, cattle, goats, and horses, as she can count of each without heaving or drawing in her breath. But remember, that if you prove unkind to her at any time and strike her three times without a cause, she shall return to me, and shall bring all her stock with her.'

Such was the marriage settlement, to which the young man gladly assented, and the bride was desired to count the number of sheep she was to have. She immediately adopted the mode of counting by fives, thus: One, two, three, four, five, one, two, three, four, five; as many times as possible in rapid succession, till her breath was exhausted. The same process of reckoning had to determine the number of goats, cattle, and horses, respectively; and in an instant the full number of each came out of the lake, when called upon by the Father.

The young couple were then married, and went to reside at a farm called Esgair Llaethdy, near Myddvai, where they lived in prosperity and happiness for several years, and became the parents of three beautiful sons.

Once upon a time there was a christening in the neighbourhood to which the parents were invited. When the day arrived the wife appeared reluctant to attend the christening, alleging that the distance was too great for her to walk. Her husband told her to fetch one of the horses from the field.

'I will,' said she, 'if you will bring me my gloves which I left in our house.'

He went for the gloves, and finding she had not gone for the horse, he playfully slapped her shoulder with one of them, saying, '*Dôs, dôs*, go, go,' when she reminded him of the terms on which she consented to marry him, and warned him to be more cautious in the future, as he had now given her one causeless blow.

On another occasion when they were together at a wedding and the assembled guests were greatly enjoying themselves the wife burst into tears and sobbed most piteously. Her husband touched her on the shoulder and inquired the cause of her weeping; she said, 'Now people are entering into trouble, and your troubles are likely to commence, as you have the *second* time stricken me without a cause.'

Years passed on, and their children had grown up, and were particularly clever young men. Amidst so many worldly blessings the husband almost forgot that only *one* causeless blow would destroy his prosperity. Still he was watchful lest any trivial occurrence should take place which his wife must regard as a breach of their marriage contract. She told him that her affection for him was unabated, and warned him to be careful lest through inadvertence he might give the last and only blow which, by an unalterable destiny, over which she had no control, would separate them forever.

One day it happened that they went to a funeral together, where, in the midst of mourning and grief at the house of the deceased, she appeared in the gayest of spirits, and indulged in inconsiderate fits of laughter, which so shocked her husband that he touched her, saying – 'Hush! hush! don't laugh.'

She said that she laughed because people when they die go out of trouble, and rising up, she went out of the house, saying, 'The last blow has been struck, our marriage contract is broken, and at an end. Farewell!'

Then she started off towards Esgair Llaethdy, where she called her cattle and other stock together, each by name, not forgetting, the 'little black calf' which had been slaughtered and was suspended on the hook, and away went the calf and all the stock with the Lady across Myddvai Mountain, and disappeared beneath the waters of the lake whence the Lady had come. The four oxen that were ploughing departed, drawing after them the plough, which made a furrow in the ground, and which remains as a testimony of the truth of this story.

She is said to have appeared to her sons, and accosting Rhiwallon, her firstborn, to have informed him that he was to be a benefactor to mankind, through healing all manner of their diseases, and she furnished him with prescriptions and instructions for the preservation of health. Then, promising to meet him when her counsel was most needed, she vanished. On several other occasions she met her sons, and pointed out to them plants and herbs, and revealed to them their medicinal qualities or virtues.

So ends the Myddvai Legend.

From: Welsh Folk-Lore

The Happy Prince

HIGH ABOVE THE city, on a tall column, stood the statue of the Happy Prince. He was gilded all over with thin leaves of fine gold, for eyes he had two bright sapphires, and a large red ruby glowed on his sword hilt.

He was very much admired indeed.

'He is as beautiful as a weathercock,' remarked one of the town councillors who wished to gain a reputation for having artistic tastes; 'only not quite so useful,' he added, fearing lest people should think him unpractical, which he really was not.

'Why can't you be like the Happy Prince?' asked a sensible mother of her little boy who was crying for the moon. 'The Happy Prince never dreams of crying for anything.'

'I am glad there is someone in the world who is quite happy,' muttered a disappointed man as he gazed at the wonderful statue.

'He looks just like an angel,' said the charity children as they came out of the cathedral in their bright scarlet cloaks and their clean white pinafores.

'How do you know?' said the mathematical master, 'you have never seen one.'

'Ah! But we have, in our dreams,' answered the children; and the mathematical master frowned and looked very severe, for he did not approve of children dreaming.

One night there flew over the city a little swallow. His friends had gone away to Egypt six weeks before, but he had stayed behind, for he was in love with the most beautiful reed. He had met her early in the spring as he was flying down the river after a big yellow moth, and had been so attracted by her slender waist that he had stopped to talk to her.

'Shall I love you?' said the swallow, who liked to come to the point at once, and the reed made him a low bow. So he flew round and round her, touching the water with his wings, and making silver ripples. This was his courtship, and it lasted all through the summer.

'It is a ridiculous attachment,' twittered the other swallows; 'she has no money, and far too many relations'; and indeed the river was quite full of reeds. Then, when the autumn came they all flew away.

After they had gone he felt lonely, and began to tire of his lady love.

'She has no conversation,' he said, 'and I am afraid that she is a coquette, for she is always flirting with the wind.'

And certainly, whenever the wind blew, the reed made the most graceful curtseys.

'I admit that she is domestic,' he continued, 'but I love travelling, and my wife, consequently, should love travelling also.'

'Will you come away with me?' he said finally to her; but the reed shook her head, she was so attached to her home.

'You have been trifling with me,' he cried. 'I am off to the pyramids. Good-bye!' and he flew away.

All day long he flew, and at night-time he arrived at the city.

'Where shall I put up?' he said; 'I hope the town has made preparations.'

Then he saw the statue on the tall column.

'I will put up there,' he cried; 'it is a fine position, with plenty of fresh air.'

So he alighted just between the feet of the Happy Prince.

'I have a golden bedroom,' he said softly to himself as he looked round, and he prepared to go to sleep; but just as he was putting his head under his wing a large drop of water fell on him.

'What a curious thing!' he cried; 'there is not a single cloud in the sky, the stars are quite clear and bright, and yet it is raining. The climate in the north of Europe is really dreadful. The Reed used to like the rain, but that was merely her selfishness.'

Then another drop fell.

'What is the use of a statue if it cannot keep the rain off?' he said; 'I must look for a good chimney pot,' and he determined to fly away.

But before he had opened his wings, a third drop fell, and he looked up, and saw – Ah! what did he see?

The eyes of the Happy Prince were filled with tears, and tears were running down his golden cheeks. His face was so beautiful in the moonlight that the little swallow was filled with pity.

'Who are you?' he said.

'I am the Happy Prince.'

'Why are you weeping then?' asked the swallow; 'you have quite drenched me.'

'When I was alive and had a human heart,' answered the statue, 'I did not know what tears were, for I lived in the Palace of Sans-Souci, where sorrow is not allowed to enter. In the daytime I played with my companions in the garden, and in the evening I led the dance in the great hall. Round the garden ran a very lofty wall, but I never cared to ask what lay beyond it, everything about me was so beautiful. My courtiers called me the Happy Prince, and happy indeed I was, if pleasure be happiness. So I lived, and so I died. And now that I am dead they have set me up here so high that I can see all the ugliness and all the misery of my city, and though my heart is made of lead yet I cannot chose but weep.'

'What! Is he not solid gold?' said the swallow to himself. He was too polite to make any personal remarks out loud.

'Far away,' continued the statue in a low musical voice, 'far away in a little street there is a poor house. One of the windows is open, and through it I can see a woman seated at a table. Her face is thin and worn, and she has coarse, red hands, all pricked by the needle, for she is a seamstress. She is embroidering passionflowers on a satin gown for the loveliest of the Queen's maids-of-honour to wear at the next court ball. In a bed in the corner of the room her little boy is lying ill. He has a fever, and is asking for oranges. His mother has nothing to give him but river water, so he is crying. Swallow, swallow, little swallow, will you not bring her the ruby out of my sword hilt? My feet are fastened to this pedestal and I cannot move.'

'I am waited for in Egypt,' said the swallow.

'My friends are flying up and down the Nile, and talking to the large lotus flowers. Soon they will go to sleep in the tomb of the great king. The king is there himself in his painted coffin. He is wrapped in yellow linen, and embalmed with spices. Round his neck is a chain of pale green jade, and his hands are like withered leaves.'

'Swallow, swallow, little swallow,' said the prince, 'will you not stay with me for one night, and be my messenger? The boy is so thirsty, and the mother so sad.'

'I don't think I like boys,' answered the swallow. 'Last summer, when I was staying on the river, there were two rude boys, the miller's sons, who were always throwing stones at me. They never hit me, of course; we swallows fly far too well for that, and besides, I come of a family famous for its agility; but still, it was a mark of disrespect.'

But the Happy Prince looked so sad that the little swallow was sorry.

'It is very cold here,' he said; 'but I will stay with you for one night, and be your messenger.'

'Thank you, little swallow,' said the prince.

So the swallow picked out the great ruby from the prince's sword, and flew away with it in his beak over the roofs of the town.

He passed by the cathedral tower, where the white marble angels were sculptured. He passed by the palace and heard the sound of dancing. A beautiful girl came out on the balcony with her lover.

'How wonderful the stars are,' he said to her, 'and how wonderful is the power of love!'

'I hope my dress will be ready in time for the state ball,' she answered; 'I have ordered passionflowers to be embroidered on it; but the seamstresses are so lazy.'

He passed over the river, and saw the lanterns hanging to the masts of the ships. He passed over the ghetto, and saw the old neighbours bargaining with each other, and weighing out money in copper scales.

At last he came to the poor house and looked in. The boy was tossing feverishly on his bed, and the mother had fallen asleep, she was so tired. In he hopped, and laid the great ruby on the table beside the woman's thimble. Then he flew gently round the bed, fanning the boy's forehead with his wings.

'How cool I feel,' said the boy,

'I must be getting better'; and he sank into a delicious slumber.

Then the swallow flew back to the Happy Prince, and told him what he had done.

'It is curious,' he remarked, 'but I feel quite warm now, although it is so cold.'

'That is because you have done a good action,' said the Prince. And the little swallow began to think, and then he fell asleep. Thinking always made him sleepy.

When day broke he flew down to the river and had a bath.

'What a remarkable phenomenon,' said the professor of ornithology as he was passing over the bridge.

'A swallow in winter!'

And he wrote a long letter about it to the local newspaper. Everyone quoted it, it was full of so many words that they could not understand.

'Tonight I go to Egypt,' said the swallow, and he was in high spirits at the prospect. He visited all the public monuments, and sat a long time on top of the church steeple. Wherever he went the sparrows chirruped, and said to each other,

'What a distinguished stranger!' so he enjoyed himself very much.

When the moon rose he flew back to the Happy Prince.

'Have you any commissions for Egypt?' he cried; 'I am just starting.'

'Swallow, swallow, little swallow,' said the Prince, 'will you not stay with me one night longer?'

'I am waited for in Egypt,' answered the swallow.

'Tomorrow my friends will fly up to the second cataract. The river-horse couches there among the bulrushes, and on a great granite throne sits the God Memnon. All night long he watches the stars, and when the morning star shines he utters one cry of joy, and then he is silent. At noon the yellow lions come down to the water's edge to drink. They have eyes like green beryl, and their roar is louder than the roar of the cataract.'

'Swallow, swallow, little swallow,' said the prince, 'far away across the city I see a young man in a garret. He is leaning over a desk covered with papers, and in a tumbler by his side there is a bunch of withered violets. His hair is brown and crisp, and his lips are red as a pomegranate, and he has large and dreamy eyes. He is trying to finish a play for the director of the theatre, but he is too cold to write any more. There is no fire in the grate, and hunger has made him faint.'

'I will wait with you one night longer,' said the swallow, who really had a good heart. 'Shall I take him another ruby?'

'Alas! I have no ruby now,' said the prince; 'my eyes are all that I have left. They are made of rare sapphires, which were brought out of India a thousand years ago. Pluck out one of them and take it to him. He will sell it to the jeweller, and buy food and firewood, and finish his play.'

'Dear Prince,' said the swallow, 'I cannot do that'; and he began to weep.

'Swallow, swallow, little swallow,' said the prince, 'do as I command you.'

So the swallow plucked out the prince's eye, and flew away to the student's garret. It was easy enough to get in, as there was a hole in the roof. Through this he darted, and came into the room. The young man had his head buried in his hands, so he did not hear the flutter of the bird's wings, and when he looked up he found the beautiful sapphire lying on the withered violets.

'I am beginning to be appreciated,' he cried; 'this is from some great admirer. Now I can finish my play,' and he looked quite happy.

The next day the swallow flew down to the harbour. He sat on the mast of a large vessel and watched the sailors hauling big chests out of the hold with ropes.

'Heave ahoy!' they shouted as each chest came up.

'I am going to Egypt'! cried the swallow, but nobody minded, and when the moon rose he flew back to the Happy Prince.

'I am come to bid you good-bye,' he cried.

'Swallow, swallow, little swallow,' said the prince, 'will you not stay with me one night longer?'

'It is winter,' answered the swallow, 'and the chill snow will soon be here. In Egypt the sun is warm on the green palm trees, and the crocodiles lie in the mud and look lazily about them. My companions are building a nest in the Temple of Baalbec, and the pink and white doves are watching them, and cooing to each other. Dear prince, I must leave you, but I will never forget you, and next spring I will bring you back two beautiful jewels in place of those you have given away. The ruby shall be redder than a red rose, and the sapphire shall be as blue as the great sea.'

'In the square below,' said the Happy Prince, 'there stands a little match-girl. She has let her matches fall in the gutter, and they are all spoiled. Her father will beat her if she does not bring home some money, and she is crying. She has no shoes or stockings, and her little head is bare. Pluck out my other eye, and give it to her, and her father will not beat her.'

'I will stay with you one night longer,' said the swallow, 'but I cannot pluck out your eye. You would be quite blind then.'

'Swallow, swallow, little swallow,' said the prince, 'do as I command you.'

So he plucked out the prince's other eye, and darted down with it. He swooped past the match-girl, and slipped the jewel into the palm of her hand.

'What a lovely bit of glass,' cried the little girl; and she ran home, laughing.

Then the swallow came back to the prince.

'You are blind now,' he said, 'so I will stay with you always.'

'No, little swallow,' said the poor prince, 'you must go away to Egypt.'

'I will stay with you always,' said the swallow, and he slept at the prince's feet.

All the next day he sat on the Prince's shoulder, and told him stories of what he had seen in strange lands. He told him of the red ibises, who stand in long rows on the banks of the Nile, and catch gold-fish in their beaks; of the sphinx, who is as old as the world itself, and lives in the desert, and knows everything; of the merchants, who walk slowly by the side of their camels, and carry amber beads in their hands; of the king of the Mountains of the Moon, who is as black as ebony, and worships a large crystal; of the great green snake that sleeps in a palm tree, and has twenty priests to feed it with honey-cakes; and of the pygmies who sail over a big lake on large flat leaves, and are always at war with the butterflies.

'Dear little swallow,' said the prince, 'you tell me of marvellous things, but more marvellous than anything is the suffering of men and of women. There is no mystery so great as misery. Fly over my city, little swallow, and tell me what you see there.'

So the swallow flew over the great city, and saw the rich making merry in their beautiful houses, while the beggars were sitting at the gates. He flew into dark lanes, and saw the white faces of starving children looking out listlessly at the black streets. Under the archway of a bridge two little boys were lying in one another's arms to try and keep themselves warm.

'How hungry we are!' they said.

'You must not lie here,' shouted the watchman, and they wandered out into the rain.

Then he flew back and told the prince what he had seen.

'I am covered with fine gold,' said the prince, 'you must take it off, leaf by leaf, and give it to my poor; the living always think that gold can make them happy.'

Leaf after leaf of the fine gold the swallow picked off, till the Happy Prince looked quite dull and grey. Leaf after leaf of the fine gold he brought to the poor, and the children's faces grew rosier, and they laughed and played games in the street.

'We have bread now!' they cried.

Then the snow came, and after the snow came the frost. The streets looked as if they were made of silver, they were so bright and glistening; long icicles like crystal daggers hung down from the eaves of the houses, everybody went about in furs, and the little boys wore scarlet caps and skated on the ice.

The poor little swallow grew colder and colder, but he would not leave the prince, he loved him too well. He picked up crumbs outside the baker's door when the baker was not looking and tried to keep himself warm by flapping his wings.

But at last he knew that he was going to die. He had just strength to fly up to the Prince's shoulder once more.

'Goodbye, dear prince!' he murmured, 'will you let me kiss your hand?'

'I am glad that you are going to Egypt at last, little swallow,' said the prince, 'you have stayed too long here; but you must kiss me on the lips, for I love you.'

'It is not to Egypt that I am going,' said the swallow. 'I am going to the House of Death. Death is the brother of Sleep, is he not?'

And he kissed the Happy Prince on the lips, and fell down dead at his feet.

At that moment a curious crack sounded inside the statue, as if something had broken. The fact is that the leaden heart had snapped right in two. It certainly was a dreadfully hard frost.

Early the next morning the mayor was walking in the square below in company with the town councillors. As they passed the column he looked up at the statue: 'Dear me! how shabby the Happy Prince looks!' he said.

'How shabby indeed!' cried the town councillors, who always agreed with the mayor; and they went up to look at it.

'The ruby has fallen out of his sword, his eyes are gone, and he is golden no longer,' said the mayor in fact, 'he is little better than a beggar!'

'Little better than a beggar,' said the town councillors.

'And here is actually a dead bird at his feet!' continued the mayor. 'We must really issue a proclamation that birds are not to be allowed to die here.'

And the town clerk made a note of the suggestion.

So they pulled down the statue of the Happy Prince.

'As he is no longer beautiful, he is no longer useful,' said the art professor at the University.

Then they melted the statue in a furnace, and the mayor held a meeting of the corporation to decide what was to be done with the metal.

'We must have another statue, of course,' he said, 'and it shall be a statue of myself.'

'Of myself,' said each of the town councillors, and they quarrelled.

When I last heard of them they were quarrelling still.

'What a strange thing!' said the overseer of the workmen at the foundry.

'This broken lead heart will not melt in the furnace. We must throw it away.'

So they threw it on a dust heap where the dead swallow was also lying.

'Bring me the two most precious things in the city,' said God to one of his angels; and the angel brought him the leaden heart and the dead bird.

'You have rightly chosen,' said God, 'for in my garden of paradise this little bird shall sing for evermore, and in my city of gold the Happy Prince shall praise me.'

From: The Happy Prince & Other Tales

The Magic Turban

THERE WERE ONCE two brothers, the sons of a rich merchant, and when he died he left all his estate to be divided between them equally. This was done, and the elder at once set about trading and improving his condition, so that very soon he became twice as rich as he had been.

But the younger son had no luck. Everything he undertook failed. Moreover, he never had the heart to say no to a friend in need. So before long he was left with not a penny in his purse or a roof over his head.

In his distress he went to his elder brother and asked help of him.

'How is this?' said the elder.

'Our father left the same to both of us, and I have prospered in the world and have now become a rich man, but you have not even a roof to shelter your head or a bite to eat.'

'Well, that's a long tale,' said the younger, 'and what is done is done. But give me another chance, and it may be that this time I will succeed in the world.'

After they had talked a long time the elder brother consented to give him fifty dollars, but if he wasted that the way he had the rest of his property, he was not to come back again.

The younger brother took the money and went off with it, but it was not long before it had slipped through his fingers just the way his other money had. Before long he was back at his brother's door, asking for help again.

The older brother scolded and reproached him. He was a spendthrift and a waster. But in the end he gave him another fifty dollars, and bade him be off, and not dare to return again.

The younger brother went off with the fifty dollars and this time he was sure he would succeed with it. But his luck was still no better than it had been before. Soon it was all gone, and back he came to his brother's house.

So it went on.

The older brother could not rid himself of him. At last the elder brother, seeing there would be no peace for him as long as he remained where he was, made up his mind to sell all his possessions and take the money and journey to a far land without telling his younger brother anything about it.

This he did, but somehow or other the younger one got wind of it. He found what ship his brother was to sail on, and then he crawled aboard at night, when nobody was watching, and hid himself among the cargo.

The next day the ship set sail. Soon they were out at sea. Then the elder brother came out on deck and strutted up and down, and he rejoiced at heart that he had shaken off the younger lad and with good luck might never see him again.

But just as he thought this, whom should he see but the lad coming across the deck to meet him and give him greeting.

The elder was a sick and sorry man. It seemed there was no ridding himself of his brother. At the first port they touched he left the ship, and his brother got off with him, for he had no idea of being left behind.

The elder brother stood there on the shore and looked about him. Then he said, 'Listen, now! It is a long way to the town. Do you stay here while I go on farther, beyond yon spit of land, and see whether I can find a dwelling where I can buy us a couple of horses; for I have no wish to journey on foot.'

The younger brother was for going along too, but to this the elder would not consent. No, no; the lad was to stay there and watch a box that the elder brother had brought along. (The box had nothing in it, but this the younger brother did not know.)

So the elder brother set out and soon was out of sight, and the younger one sat on the box and kicked his heels and waited, and waited and waited and waited; but his brother never did come back.

Then the lad knew the older one had made a fool of him. He looked in the box and found it empty. So off he set to see whether he could make his own way in the world and no thanks to anyone.

He journeyed on a short way and a long way, and so he came to a place where three men were quarrelling together fiercely, and the things they were quarrelling over were an old turban, a piece of carpet, and a sword.

As soon as they saw the lad they stopped quarrelling and ran and caught hold of him.

'You shall decide! You shall decide!' they shouted all together.

'What is it you wish me to decide?' asked the lad.

Then the men told him they were three brothers, and that when their father died he had left them these three things, the turban, the carpet, and the sword. Whoever placed the turban on his head would at once become invisible. Whoever sat on the carpet had only to wish himself wherever he would be, and the carpet would carry him there in a twinkling, and the sword would cut through anything, and no magic could stand against it.

'These things should belong to me, because I am the eldest,' cried one of the men.

'No, I should have them because I am the strongest and stoutest,' said the second.

'But I am the youngest and weakest and need them most,' cried the third.

They then began to quarrel again and even came to blows.

'Stop, stop,' cried the lad. 'You said that I should decide this matter for you, so why quarrel about it? But before I decide I must try the things and see whether what you have told me is really so.'

To this the brothers agreed. First they gave him the sword, and the lad took it in his hand and aimed a blow at a rock nearby, and the sword cut through the rock as smoothly and easily as though it had been a piece of cheese.

'Now give me the turban,' said the lad.

The brothers gave him the turban, and he placed it upon his head and at once became invisible!

'Now the carpet.'

The brothers spread out the carpet on the ground, and the lad seated himself upon it with the turban still upon his head and the sword in his hand! Then he wished himself far away in some place where the brothers would never find him.

Immediately he found himself in the outskirts of a large city. He stepped from the carpet and rolled it up and took the turban from his head and looked about him. He had no idea of going back to return the things to the brothers, and if they waited for him they waited a long time.

'It will teach them not to quarrel but to live at peace with each other,' said the lad to himself.

Then he made his way to the nearest house, for he was hungry and meant to ask for a bite to eat.

He knocked, and an old woman opened the door, and she was so old that her chin and her nose met.

'Good day, mother,' said the lad.

'Good day to you,' answered the crone.

'Will you give me a bite to eat, for the love of charity?'

Yes, the crone would do that. She gave him a bite and a sup and a bit over, and while he was eating and drinking she sat and talked with him.

'What is the news here in the city?' asked the lad.

'Oh the same news as ever.'

'And what is that? For I am a stranger here and know no more of yesterday or the week before than of today.'

'Then I will tell you. Over yonder lies the castle, and the king lives there. He has only one daughter, and she is a beauty, you may believe. Every night the princess disappears from the castle, and where she goes no one can tell but herself, and she will not. So the king has offered a reward to anyone who will find out. The half of his kingdom he offers and the hand of the princess as well, if only anyone can tell him where she goes.'

'That is a good hearing,' said the lad. 'I have a mind to try for that prize myself.'

'No, but wait a bit,' said the old woman. 'There is another side to the story, for if you try and fail your head will be lifted from your shoulders with a sharp sword, and you are too fine a young man to lose your life in that way.'

But the lad was determined to try. In vain the old woman warned and entreated him. He thanked her for the meal he had eaten, and then off he set for the palace. There he told the errand that had brought him and after that it did not take long for him to get to see the king.

'So you think you can find out where the princess goes at night,' said the king.

Yes, the lad thought he could.

Very well, then, he might have a try at it, but he must remember that if he tried and failed his head would be cut from his shoulders with a sharp sword.

Yes, the lad understood that, and he was ready to take the risk.

So that night he was taken to the door of a room in a high tower, and the room was of iron and had only one door and one window. Into this room the princess was put every night, and it would be the duty of the lad to watch at the door and see either that she did not leave it, or where she went.

Presently the princess came upstairs and passed by the lad without so much as a glance, but his heart leapt within him, she was so beautiful.

She opened the door to go in, and the lad put on his turban of darkness and slipped in after her, but the princess did not know that because he was invisible. She closed the door tight and sighed three times, and then a great black demon stood before her, and he was terrible to look upon, he was so huge and ugly.

'Oh, my dear Lala,' said the princess, 'let us be off at once. I do not know why, but I feel so frightened, just as though some misfortune were about to come upon me.'

'That is nonsense,' said the demon. 'But do you seat yourself upon my head, and we will be off at once.'

The demon wore a buckler upon his head, and now he stooped, and she seated herself upon it, but the lad was quick and sprang up and took his place beside her.

'Ai! Ai!' cried the demon, 'but you are heavy today, princess.'

Then the demon flew out through the window and away through the night.

'I do not know what you mean,' answered the princess. 'I am no heavier and no lighter than I was last night.'

Then the demon flew out through the window and away through the night so fast that the lad had much ado to keep from falling off.

After a while they came to a garden, the like of which the lad had never seen before and never expected to see again, for the leaves of the trees were of silver, and the branches were of gold, and the fruits were emeralds and rubies.

As they passed through it the lad stretched out his hand and broke off a twig and put it in his bosom. Then all the trees in the garden began to sigh and moan.

'Child of man! Child of man! why do you break and torture us?'

The princess shuddered.

'Someone besides ourselves is here in the garden,' she cried.

'That cannot be, or we would see him,' answered the demon, but he was frightened and flew on faster than before.

Presently they came to another garden and it was even more wonderful than the first, for here the trees were of diamonds, and the fruits of every kind of precious stones you can think of.

As they passed through it the lad stretched out his hand and broke off a twig. Then all the trees began to sigh and moan.

'Child of man! Child of man! Why do you break and torture us?' they cried.

'Oh, my dear Lala, what did I tell you?' asked the princess. 'I am afraid'; and she trembled all over her body.

The demon answered nothing, but he flew on even faster than ever.

Soon after they came to a magnificent palace, and the demon flew in through a window and alighted. Then the princess and the lad leapt down from the buckler, and the demon was glad to have the weight off him. After that he vanished.

The princess opened a door and went into another room, with the lad close behind her, and there was the king of all the demons, and he was so huge and black that the demon Lala was nothing to him.

'My dearest dear one, why are you so late tonight?' asked he of the princess.

'I do not know what was the matter,' answered the fair one, 'but something is terribly wrong'; and she told him all that had happened.

The Demon laughed at her.

'You are nervous,' said he. 'But come! You have not kissed me yet.'

He came close to the princess to kiss her, but the lad stepped between them and gave the Demon such a push that he almost fell over; at the same time he himself gave the princess a kiss upon the cheek.

'Why do you push me away?' cried the Demon, and he was very angry.

The princess began to tremble again.

'I did not push you,' said she.

'Moreover, someone kissed me on the cheek. I am sure somebody is in the room with us.'

The King Demon looked all around, but he could see nobody. Then he called a slave to bring the princess the jewelled slippers she always wore when she came to his palace.

The slave brought the slippers on a golden cushion, and they were crusted over with pearls and precious stones. He knelt before the princess, and she took one and put it on, but at the same time the lad took the other and slipped it in his bosom. The princess and the Demon did not know what had become of it. They hunted everywhere, but they could not find it.

'There, now! See how careless you are,' said the Demon; and he bade the slave bring another pair of slippers.

This the slave did, but it was the same with this pair as with the others. While the princess was putting on one slipper the lad took the other and hid it in his bosom. The princess and the Demon and the slave all looked for it, but they could not find it.

At that the princess flew into a passion and threw both the slippers away from her.

'I do not care,' said she; 'and now I will not wear any slippers at all.'

'Never mind!' answered the Demon. 'We will have a sherbet together, and after that we will eat.'

He clapped his hands, and another slave appeared, bearing two crystal goblets full of sherbet. The princess took one goblet and the Demon the other. Just as they were about to drink the lad smote the crystal goblet from the princess's hand so that it fell upon the marble floor and was shattered, and all the sherbet was spilled.

The lad picked up a splinter of the crystal and hid it in his bosom with the golden twig, the diamond twig, and the two slippers. But the princess shook and trembled until she could hardly stand, and even the Demon was troubled.

'Why did you cast the goblet on the floor?' he asked.

'I did not,' answered the princess, 'but someone struck it from my hand'; and she began to weep.

The Demon comforted her and bade other slaves bring in the feast that had been prepared for him and the princess.

Quickly the slaves brought it and placed it before them. The lad had never seen such a feast. All the dishes were of gold and were carved to represent scenes in demon life, and the handles were set thick with precious stones and enamelled in strange colours. There were all sorts of delicious things to eat, so that the lad's mouth watered at the smell of them.

The Demon and the princess sat down to eat, but it was small good the princess got of the feast, for every time the Demon put anything on her plate the lad snatched it away and ate it, and the princess was left hungry. The lad also took one of the golden forks and one of the golden spoons and hid them in his bosom.

'What did I tell you,' cried the princess. 'Something is wrong! Something is *terribly* wrong.'

'Yes, I can see that myself,' said the King Demon. 'You had better go on home again, for we will get no pleasure out of this night, and that I can easily see.'

Lala was called, the princess mounted the buckler in haste, and away the Demon flew with her. But this time the lad did not fly with them.

He waited until they were gone, and then he drew the Sword of Sharpness and smote the King Demon's head from his shoulders.

At once a clap of thunder sounded; the castle rocked, and the walls crumbled about him. The trees in the gardens were withered, and a thick darkness fell, while all about him sounded cries and groans.

But the lad seated himself upon the carpet and wished himself back at the door of the room in the tower, and there he was in a twinkling, long before Lala had flown in through the window with the princess, even though he flew as swiftly as the wind.

The lad took off the Turban of Darkness, and rolled up the carpet, and lay down and closed his eyes as though he were asleep.

Presently the princess opened the door and peered out. There lay the lad, snoring and with his eyes closed. The princess drew a sharp needle and ran it into the lad's heel, but he never flinched, so she felt sure he was asleep.

'Thou fool!' said she scornfully. 'Sleep on, and tomorrow thou shalt pay the penalty.'

Then she went back into the room and closed the door.

The next day the princess called the guards and bade them carry the lad away and cut the head from his shoulders.

'Wait a bit,' said the lad. 'Do not be in such a hurry. First we must appear before thy father the king; he must decide in this case, and it may be I have something to tell him that will be worth the hearing.'

The princess could not refuse this, so she and the lad were brought before the king, and the lad began to tell his story. When he came to the part where the great black Demon had come and flown away with the princess she turned first as red as blood and then as pale as death.

'It is not true!' she cried, but the king bade her be silent.

Then the lad told how they had flown through the gardens.

'It is all a wicked lie,' moaned the princess, but the lad drew forth the twigs he had broken from the trees and showed them to the king as proof of his truth.

After that the lad told of how they had entered the castle, and how the King Demon had tried to kiss the princess, and of the shattered goblet and the uneaten feast, and he had the splinter of crystal and the spoon and fork to show, so the king knew it was all true, and the princess looked as though she wished she were dead.

Last of all he told how the princess had returned on the Demon's buckler, and how he had remained behind and cut off the king Demon's head, and how the castle had fallen and the gardens had withered, and all had become darkness and confusion.

When the princess heard this she gave a shriek of joy.

'Then you have saved me!' she cried. 'Never again need I fly forth at night at the will of the Demon nor be his slave!'

Then it was her turn to tell her story. She told how one time the King Demon had seen her walking in the palace gardens and had fallen in love with her, and how he had used his magic to gain power over her. She told how she hated him and feared him, but how against her will he had forced her to come to visit him every night in his castle and had sent the demon Lala to fetch her. But now that the King Demon was dead, she was free, and it was the lad who had saved her.

When the king, her father, heard this, he marvelled greatly. Glad was he that such a brave lad was to be his son-in-law, for that was his promise. The lad and the princess were betrothed then and there, and the king gave orders that a grand wedding feast should be prepared, for they were to be married as soon as possible. All the good folks far and near were invited to come to the feast.

The lad's elder brother was invited with the rest, but he never dreamed that the brave lad who was to marry the princess was his own younger brother.

He came to the palace on the feast day and took his place at the table with the other guests, and then he looked up at the three thrones where the king and the princess and the lad were sitting, and there it was his own younger brother who sat there.

When the man saw that, he was afraid, for he remembered how he had deserted the lad on the seashore to live or die as fate willed, and he feared he might be punished for it.

But the younger brother bore him no grudge, but was grateful to him for what he had done.

As soon as he saw the elder one there among the guests, he sent a servant for him and placed him in the seat of honour and called him brother.

So all was happiness and rejoicing. Everybody was happy, but the lad and the princess were happiest of all, because they loved each other and had just been married.

From: Tales of Folk & Fairies

Finis

Workbooks From The Scheherazade Foundation

We hope that you have enjoyed this collection of stories, gleaned from varying cultural corners of the world, and that you have been entertained by them.

But, have you considered the deeper meanings and interwoven layers that lie hidden beneath the surface?

At The Scheherazade Foundation, we believe that Teaching-Stories contain wisdom, information, and marvels that have the power to transform the way we think, and thereby change our lives.

Employed as a bedrock of culture throughout the centuries – challenging established patterns of thinking, while passing on knowledge and values – tales such as the ones contained in this volume are a rich resource ready and waiting to be mined.

As an aid to help in the perception of less-obvious facets and layers, we have created a series of original Workbooks. Aimed at stimulating thought-provoking discussions and igniting deep reflection, these tools will assist in unlocking the power of Teaching-Stories.

www.ingramcontent.com/pod-product-compliance
Lightning Source LLC
Chambersburg PA
CBHW030234180626
46810CB00008B/3129